A Time to

Prey

Murder at Hartlebury: Inspector
Wickfield Investigates

To one who happens to be called Giles –
My Brother!

A Time to

Prey

Julius Falconer

PNEUMA SPRINGS PUBLISHING UK

First Published in 2010 by:
Pneuma Springs Publishing

A Time to Prey
Copyright © 2010 Julius Falconer
ISBN: 978-1-905809-83-7

Castle line drawing used by permission

Pneuma Springs Publishing
A Subsidiary of Pneuma Springs Ltd.
7 Groveherst Road, Dartford Kent, DA1 5JD.
E: admin@pneumasprings.co.uk
W: www.pneumasprings.co.uk

A catalogue record for this book is available from the British Library.

ONE

Do you know Hartlebury Castle, the residence of the Bishops of Worcester? It is a grand mansion - more of a stately house as it stands today than a castle in the usual sense of that word. It is, as far as you and I, who are not architectural historians, are concerned, a late-seventeenth-century creation on a thirteenth-century foundation, forming a sort of shallow U, with the remnants of a moat along the back of the house. The front looks on to a circular lawn surrounded by a tarmacked drive which deposits the visitor in front of a grand door surmounted by a lantern, a coat of arms and two stone spheres. There are shrubs, trees and virginia creeper, and the immediate surrounds of the house and grounds are the ploughed fields of timeless Worcestershire. The house is spacious: a great hall, a gallery, a library, a chapel, other public rooms, the usual offices, servants' quarters, outbuildings and so forth. If I had seen it in more auspicious circumstances, my memories would perhaps be less tinged with melancholy. The fact is that I was granted admittance only because the bishop had met an untimely death. He had, not to put too fine a point on it, been murdered.

Your informant is Stan Wickfield, a name I hope familiar to most of you as an inspector with the Worcestershire Criminal Investigation Department since 1961. I live in Worcester, am married to Beth, and have two sons, neither of them policemen. To forestall Mr Julius Falconer in the telling of this bewildering case, I have taken a stretch of extended leave, in this year of grace 1966, to put down for you the sequence of events while they are still fresh in my mind. Mr Falconer and I, I regret to tell you, have had words*. I am less bitter than I was, but since our breach is not quite mended, and far

---

* *Occasioned by his intransigence in the case of the St Mary's Court skeletons: see The Bones of Murder.*

from confident that he will do justice to the ins and outs of this case, and in particular to my own role in it, I have determined to lay the murder (and its solution!) before you myself.

Probably the best starting-point is to introduce you to the bishop's household, by which I mean his wife, his chaplain, his secretary, his almoner and his housekeeper. There is also an archdeacon who will claim our attention. I list these here in the order in which we happened to interview them on that first morning, and I ascribe no further significance to it. Furthermore, you will forgive me, I trust, from confirming or denying that one of these household members was responsible for the death. You see, I wish you to view matters as Sergeant Hewitt and I viewed them, and we came to the case without preconceptions of any kind, prepared to consider an intimate of the bishop, a casual acquaintance, a complete stranger, an insider or an outsider, as the perpetrator; no possibility was barred. I shall give you neither more nor less than all the information we had at our disposal (including the crucial clue that I failed to spot at the time), as it came to us.

Mrs Wyndham-Brookes, the bishop's significant other, was a stately woman in her fifties, whose twin goals in life were to sustain her husband's position in society and to bask in its glow. I trust that you will not take this remark in a derogatory spirit: there are, after all, such things as justifiable pride and Christian self-love. I should not wish you to cast Mrs Wyndham-Brookes in the mould of Mrs Proudie, who was in any case a fictional character. Mrs Wyndham-Brookes, née Sybil Scrutton, had met her husband when he was a humble curate in the rural parish of St Peter's, Martley, to the west of Worcester, and, divining that he was marked out for preferment, cultivated his acquaintance assiduously. Actually, I must take myself to task there. The investigation of Bishop Wyndham-Brookes' death led me to dislike his relict, for no rational reason that I could lay before you, and I urge you to take no notice of remarks from my pen that might be taken to be disparaging in her regard. (Furthermore, she displayed a tender side later in our investigation, and I had occasion to revise my initial opinions – to some extent.) I could just as easily, and perhaps should, have told you that from their earliest meeting she determined to submerge her own ambitions in order to promote the evident virtues of young Mr Wyndham-Brookes in the service of his (and her) Church: a noble self-sacrifice – except that that is not quite how matters occurred!

I understand from people who study these matters that one's self-image, one's understanding of one's own person, is intimately linked with one's body: its shape, its size, its appearance. Do you wish that your ears were smaller? that your nose were a little less snub? that your legs were sturdier? that you presented an altogether more pleasing aspect to the world at large? Then you need counselling. Mrs Wyndham-Brookes, on the other hand, was entirely satisfied with her appearance. Her dignified, even regal, bulk was the fitting embodiment of an imposing and majestic spirit that tolerated little opposition from mortals whose position in society placed them below that of bishop. Conversely, she fawned on the titled and the privileged. This was because she recognised, by instinct and by experience, that the titled and the privileged were the movers in society and in the Church, and that it was therefore they who could, if properly cultivated and encouraged, ensure the continuance of the Church as the permanent presence of Christ's Body in British society.

I have come to appreciate, in the course of a so far short but, um, distinguished career, that at the start of a case, everybody is suspect. This is the only attitude that encourages alertness in the investigating officers. It was, very early on, borne in on us that Mrs Wyndham-Brookes was a disappointed and frustrated woman. You must wonder why the see of Worcester, and with it Hartlebury Castle as a private residence, should not measure up to almost anyone's ambitions. The truth is that Sybil Wyndham-Brookes had begun to nourish ambitions to be the wife of an archbishop, of which there are only two in the Church of England. Pictures of Bishopthorpe Palace and even Lambeth Palace floated increasingly before her mind's eye, her husband a person of the greatest consequence in the divine order of things, and she herself a fitting spouse at his side. Now Bishop Wyndham-Brookes had, with Worcester, exhausted his allocation of ambition. More than that, he was losing fire. At over sixty, he was beginning to wonder whether an early retirement might not suit him best, whereas his consort had no intention of being put out to grass in mere middle age. If she were suddenly to find herself a widow, she would be free to set her cap at Bishop Boyde of Colchester, who was considered by many to be most eligible for the see of York. I suppose, to do the lady justice, that such ideas were unformulated, possibly hidden even from herself, but I teased them out for myself in the course of our investigation – I was in any case mistaken in my supposition. Her aim was not to promote herself but to put her gifts unflinchingly at the Church's service, even if, by divine fiat, it meant changing horses mid-stream (if one may so express it without disrespect). So much for the moment for Mrs Wyndham-Brookes. Let us pass on to the bishop's chaplain.

The Reverend David Skyner was a tall, powerfully-built individual whose talents included cricket, ancient languages and the pianoforte. His muscular frame and impressive height would have given him influence even if they had not been matched by an active and forceful personality. He had been proud to be chosen to be the bishop's chaplain, because the position gave him access to ecclesiastical personages of every kind and level and to the inner councils of the great and good. I should perhaps explain that, as I saw it, the Bishop of Worcester's chaplain was more than a confidant: he was an *alter ego*, supporting the bishop with advice, encouragement and information. He acted as a sounding-board, a purveyor (to the bishop's discreet ear) of rumour, a point of contact, a confessor, a theologian: in short, a right-hand man. Mrs Wyndham-Brookes did not resent his influence over her husband, because, firstly, she recognised his gifts, in many ways superior to her own, and, secondly, she saw that he kept the bishop's courage screwed to the sticking-post.

Mr Skyner was from a professional North Country family, steeped in the unforgiving climate of Northumberland and the traditions of catholic Anglicanism. He had prospered at school, gone on to Queen's College, Edgbaston, for his theological training – there was no reason why a high churchman should not attend an ecumenical college, if only to broaden his outlook! - and been appointed assistant curate in his home diocese of Durham. Eventually, when still in his thirties, he had been appointed to his present post, and his discretion, industry and theological agility (accompanied by a firm grasp of Roman doctrines) had endeared him to his master. Did I like Mr Skyner? I shall not furnish an answer, to demonstrate to you that I was impartial in my approach to the case, but I can tell you that I came to regard him as a suspect because of his undoubted ambition. Bishop Wyndham-Brookes was going no further in the Church. If he soldiered on for a year or two, at his wife's behest, and then retired to a country parish, Mr Skyner's calculation was that his own days as an episcopal candidate with good prospects were over. If, however, the see fell vacant all of a sudden, the bishop's chaplain, who doubled up as vicar general, would naturally step into the breach, and who could tell to what that might lead? I admit that this was all speculation on my part. I also speculated that Mr Skyner was growing increasingly frustrated by Bishop Wyndham-Brookes' lack of dynamism, and that the stagnation was straining his composure.

May I add a comment at this point? I should not like you to suppose that to suspect a character in the drama is to do him or her an injustice. I was prepared to take everyone I met at face value, but it would have been foolish to refuse to realise that even the seemingly most exemplary citizen is capable of murder. Few citizens exhibit the mark of Cain on their foreheads. Mrs Wyndham-Brookes and Mr Skyner were to all appearances above suspicion; but what if I came to that same conclusion about *all* the people in this case?

The bishop's secretary was another clergyman, a Mr Simon Stringer. He was responsible for the bishop's diary, correspondence and public functions: a busy man. Unlike the bishop's chaplain, Mr Stringer tended to the evangelical wing (or branch, or section, or trend – I leave you, gentle reader, to select your own term) of the Anglican Church. He felt that fidelity to the Bible was the anchor by which the Church could stay firm in a sea of troubles, and that niceness in the matters of vestment, ritual and devotion ill became a serious Christian. On the other hand, one would wish to add that his theology was not so erudite as the chaplain's.

Mr Stringer was married and had a family. He did not therefore reside at Hartlebury Castle but reported for work each week-day morning and left at the conclusion of the working day to return to the bosom of his adoring family. He was a somewhat melancholy man, imbued with a sense, not exactly of the futility or emptiness of life, but of life's precariousness. We are balanced on a cliff's edge, he thought, to be precipitated down the abyss by the inscrutable manoeuvres of history if they were that way inclined. This did not imply, on the secretary's part, a lack of trust in God, since God would use the fall (if such there should be) to open up new vistas and theatres of action, and he would in any case offer his continued support in the new circumstances, but it nonetheless brought to Mr Stringer's daily business a piquancy that betrayed itself in restrained efficiency that lacked humour.

You may well be asking yourself why on earth I should come to regard this hardworking, respectable, gentle man as a candidate for the role of murderer. Allow me to explain. Mr Stringer, at the bishop's right hand in the organisation of the bishop's diocesan duties and responsibilities, was the quiet and efficient counterbalance to the more extravert chaplain - also on the episcopal right hand! - but his silent subservience concealed his constant fear of dismissal. He knew that, as a professed evangelical, he did not enjoy his lordship's theological favour and that he was therefore a concession to the Church's Bible-based constituency on (as we might put it) the left wing. I did not know at the time that there was a lot more to his fear than this would suggest, but you will learn more of that in its place. He regarded his position as secretary, not exactly as a sinecure, but certainly as a desirable billet, given his shyness, his introversion, his lack of ease in public speaking. I guessed that he also knew, by intuition, I supposed, that Mrs Wyndham-Brookes was attempting to oust him, and in his lack of self-esteem he felt that he would not secure another living and would be unable to provide for his sick wife and his children. He could doubtless hope for a less catholic successor to Bishop Wyndham-Brookes. I did not regard murder of the bishop as a *likely* option on Stringer's part, but I stored it away as a possibility.

The bishop's almoner was of another stamp. I am sorry to have to tell you that, having no idea what an almoner did, I was obliged to make inquiries. Sparing you the historical background to the office, I can tell you, in straightforward, twentieth-century parlance, that an almoner is responsible for a bishop's charitable giving. Perhaps not every bishop employs one. The late Bishop of Worcester did. Now charitable giving is a moral minefield. It would be the easiest feat in the world to divest oneself of all one's assets by simply giving them away, to feed the poor, to relieve distress, to succour the wretched, but few religions have counselled it: partly, I have no doubt, because to give away all your goods is effectively to deprive you of any chance to help others in the future and to render yourself a burden on others, or at least a recipient of charity, in your turn. Judaism encourages the gift of a tithe annually to poor Jews, but the more normal figure, I understand, is 5% or 6%. Islam imposes a duty on its adherents to give $2^{1/2}$% of a stated portion of their assets each year to Muslim charities. Christianity has at times and in places unofficially urged 10% as an ideal to aim for. Often the decision is left to the individual giver, in the light of personal circumstances. The United Kingdom donates something like 0.03% of its gross national product every year to poor countries. However, I digress. I did not inquire about Bishop Wyndham-Brookes' precise policy in this area, but I suspect that the fact that he had engaged an almoner indicated, not his reluctance to be personally involved, but his determination that his almsgiving should be placed on an efficient and businesslike footing. Mr Havelock Blake, like the secretary, lived outside the castle. He came in two or three times a week to peruse requests from parishes and the many begging letters that land up on a bishop's desk. Having sifted through them and decided to respond on the basis of certain principles - he was to show compassion, understanding and discretion, he was to guard against deception, he was to make further inquiries where necessary, his letters were to be sensitive, he was to adhere to a strict budget, and so forth – he would draft the replies and prepare cheques for the bishop's signature. It was all conducted in as personal a way as was compatible with Christian prudence, common sense and efficiency.

The bishop's almoner, Mr Blake, a thin, balding man in his fifties, was a disappointment to himself. He had embarked on life with optimism and high aspirations, but a characteristic reserve had kept him from achieving high office, from finding a wife, from making his mark in the pulpit or in scholarship, from, in short being noticed by anyone who mattered. Not his personality, only his unobtrusive efficiency, had commended him to Bishop Wyndham-Brookes as the instrument of the episcopal charitable purse. Havelock Blake was the product of a conventional working-class environment in the sizeable Midland brewing town of Burton on Trent, but to outline his path thence to the post of almoner to the Bishop of Worcester is not to our purpose. Suffice it to say that Mr Blake was worthy but dull. This is not a moral judgement, merely a statement of fact. I began to suspect him of murder when I realised, to my surprise, that he was desperate to marry Mrs Wyndham-Brookes! I think she would not have reciprocated any advances on his part: as we have seen, her dreams for the future were pitched higher than a bishop's humble almoner; but that would not have prevented his rash attempt to engage her affections, once her husband was removed from the scene – I surmised.

The housekeeper at Hartlebury Castle, a residential post, was filled by a mild lady with the sonorous name of Myrtle Wedlake, a widow of, shall we say, middle age, whom the bishop had inherited, so to speak, from a previous incumbent at Hartlebury Castle. Not having an army of servants at her disposal, she did most of the work herself, but eight hours a day were sufficient for her needs and for those of the bishop's household and guests. She laboured away, allocating the charlady her duties for the day, arranging flowers, making beds, ordering kitchen supplies, cooking and so forth. She answered to the bishop's wife. Her secret, which I can share with you because it came out in the course of our inquiries, is that she nourished an extreme fondness for the bishop's almoner and hoped one day to persuade him to reciprocate. I regarded this eventuality as highly unlikely, but it was not my place to say so. By then it was too late anyway, since I had passed out of their lives.

11

Mrs Wedlake feared for her position. She was reprimanded by Mrs Wyndham-Brookes for some minor misdemeanour, and in the course of this carpeting, Mrs Wyndham-Brookes let slip, accidentally on purpose, one presumes, the information that the bishop had considered terminating Mrs Wedlake's employment in favour of someone less given to fluster and panic. This move would have cast the housekeeper on to a strange and daunting world outside the confines of Hartlebury Castle, and that was not a prospect to be countenanced. I do not intend to give you the impression that Mrs Wedlake never left the castle. She had family in Worcestershire and elsewhere, with whom she spent her days off or her holidays: a sister, nieces and a nephew, several cousins, an ancient aunt in a retirement home. She patronised shops in Kidderminster and Stourport; she used the services of the local library in Stourport; she attended the dentist, the optician and the doctor in the towns. Her working life and her interests, however, were centred on the daily round at Hartlebury: familiar, satisfying, soothing. It was her life.

Finally to our archdeacon. An archdeacon, I came to understand, is a representative of the bishop in a subdivision of the diocese called, naturally, an archdeaconry, which consists of clusters of parishes called deaneries. (Are you still with me?) He is usually, and he was in this case, an episcopal appointee, chosen from among clergy who have successfully completed six years of ministry. His responsibilities cover the administration of Church property, the disciplinary supervision of the clergy, the induction of vicars, the admission of church wardens and the proper conduct of public worship. In the diocese of Worcester, there are, I learned, two archdeacons, the archdeacon of Worcester being the only one whom we met in the course of our investigation. (The other one, I came to understand, was away at the time.) His name was Maddock Rolfe, and he hailed originally from London. Mr Rolfe was in his early to mid-thirties, with an imposing forehead and a shock of black hair, protruding teeth, a broken nose and a sallow, unhealthy complexion. What he lacked in personal appearance I am sure he more than compensated for by way of saintliness, patience, fortitude and a score of other Christian virtues. He was a happily married man, with two small girls on whom he doted. Even though he was one of those rarer mortals who occasionally asked himself Big Questions (and, like all such, came away puzzled), this did not prevent him from contributing manfully to the prosperity and success of the Church of his baptism by labouring in the Lord's vineyard to the best of his ability. Unfortunately he suffered, not exactly a mid-life crisis but, let us say, a change of heart, which set him at loggerheads with his bishop. It came about in this way.

A few months before the bishop's death, Mr Rolfe pottered up to London to hear Dr Martyn Lloyd-Jones preach at Westminster Chapel, where he had been pastor for over twenty years. The archdeacon did so not out of contumely, on the supposition that he was betraying the traditions of his youth, but out of curiosity. He was bowled over by the preacher's fervour and sincerity, by the enthusiasm and adulation of the congregation, and above all the rightness of his cause. Matters might have rested there, for Mr Rolfe, if, a few weeks later, Dr Lloyd-Jones had not caused controversy by publicly calling on evangelicals to quit their Church in favour of denominations which were more Bible-based. This trumpet-call did not fall on deaf ears in the Rolfe household in distant Worcestershire, where the archdeacon resolved that his response was to be, not his resignation, as Dr Lloyd-Jones purposed, but nothing less than the bishop's removal. All this animosity, at such a high-flown theological and executive level, was new to me, I confess, and you must bear with me if, in the course of our inquiries, I had for the most part to feel my way.

You may have come to the – mistaken - conclusion, patient reader, that I found myself in, as it were, a typical country-house murder-mystery, where the suspects are necessarily limited to the circle of guests, a sort of clerical *Mousetrap*. May I disabuse you? If I have chosen to list the chief members of the Bishop of Worcester's household in this opening chapter, it is only because that is where Hewitt and I necessarily began. I came to realise, however, that the ramifications of the case were numerous and unpredictable.

TWO

When news of the bishop's death came through, Sergeant Hewitt and I drove out post haste to Hartlebury Castle to begin our investigation. It was a cool autumn morning with the promise of some warmth later on as the mists cleared. The ten-mile journey on the A449 was pleasant if unexciting. Bevere Lane, Egg Lane, Lock Lane, Sinton Lane and other country roads tempted us to diverge from our chosen path of official business, but Hewitt drove determinedly on until we drew up at the front of the castle. We had hardly had time to get our bearings and admire the architecture, which I had not seen before, when a tall, lanky clergyman, doleful of countenance, stepped out to meet us.

'Stringer,' he announced. 'I'm the bishop's secretary. I'm so very sorry you've been called out, inspector, but we're making quite sure we do the right thing. Oh, dear, I fear the worst. I can't understand it, I just can't understand it.'

He muttered away to himself, shaking his head, as he stood aside to wave us into the hall. The great hall at Hartlebury is an impressive and elegant space, east-facing, with three large gothickesque windows (later modifications, I understand) giving on to the front lawn. The arched roof, made with timbers donated (it is averred) by King Richard II, reaches up the full height of the building. To your left as you enter the front door is the door into the salon (I prefer this term to 'saloon', which I believe was its official title); to your right, at the far end of the hall, is a gracious double staircase leading into the north wing. It was in the great hall that Hewitt and I conducted our initial interviews. We ascertained from the secretary that, apart from the bishop and his wife, only the chaplain and the housekeeper slept on the premises, but that the secretary himself, the almoner and the archdeacon had offices there which they might occupy at hours of their choice.

The first member of the household whom we asked to see was the sorrowing widow. I always regard these preliminary interviews as an ambivalent exercise. Of course, there has to be a first interview, but the guilty party is sometimes more likely to betray him or herself later on, when our grasp of the situation is, one hopes, firmer and maturer. In the opening skirmish, as it were, the murderer is cautious; the contradictions and incoherences emerge only later, when the murderer has had time and possibly also occasion to change details of his or her story in the light of our progressive mastery of the case (again, I speak hypothetically!). Accordingly, when Mrs Sybil Wyndham-Brookes took the stage, I was not necessarily expecting dramatic revelations. Mr Stringer escorted her into our presence and then discreetly disappeared. The widow was not in black, but she was soberly dressed, without jewellery apart from her wedding-ring. The chair creaked under her weight.

'Mrs Wyndham-Brookes,' I began, 'may I say how sorry we are to meet in the present melancholy circumstances?'

'It is kind of you to say so, inspector. It has certainly been a great shock.'

'Well, I can assure you that we shall do everything in our power to bring the matter to a conclusion as soon as possible. It is certainly all very mysterious at the moment, but we shall apply the full resources of the Worcestershire police-force to its solution.'

The widow acknowledged this assurance with a nod of her well-coiffed head.

'Would you be so kind as to tell us anything that may shed light on your husband's death?' I said. 'You will appreciate that at the moment we are completely in the dark.'

'Yes, of course, inspector, but I cannot promise to be very coherent. It's all been such a shock. The first thing I must tell you is that a bishop is surrounded by enemies.'

Here she looked particularly severe, with her lips pursed and her eyes glinting with intense earnestness.

'I have spent years fighting off marauders and slanderers and stiffening my husband's moral fibre to resist the assaults of the foe. You see, when a man is in a position of such authority and importance as my husband was, he is the target of the envious and the ambitious, the resentful and the indignant, the petty-minded and the bitter, the foolish, the blinkered and the sheerly wicked. His murder comes as no surprise to me, I have to tell you. I suppose it was only a matter of time before Satan had his evil way with a man of such influence and Christian charity who was advancing the

Kingdom of God daily through his good works, and diligence, and impressive piety.'

The relict paused here to contemplate (I presumed) her husband's noble career ignobly cut short. I might add that throughout her little speech she addressed *me,* as if a mere sergeant was beneath her notice.

'Of course, I can't tell you who was responsible for this act of barbarism. It beggars belief that anyone could stoop so low as to take the life of so fine a man in cold blood; but then history is littered with such violence. What a wicked world it is, inspector.' She sighed in the vigour of her despair.

'And now I suppose I shall have to leave this place, cast into an inhospitable world, childless and friendless and unsupported by an indifferent Church.' A few sobs followed this expression of her hopelessness.

'Now, now, Mrs Wyndham-Brookes,' I said soothingly, 'I'm quite sure your husband's friends and superiors will rally round and that you can therefore be confident of a comfortable widowhood. Can I just ask,' I said after a short pause, 'have you no suspicions at all which might point us in the right direction?' Because we were seated near the window at the centre of the room, I was quite sure that we could not be overheard.

Mrs Wyndham-Brookes nevertheless looked round her, leaned forward and spoke in a low voice.

'Inspector, I may as well tell you, although Christian charity might urge me to silence, that I have never trusted the bishop's secretary: a weak and insignificant little man, quite unsuited to his post. I just don't trust him, I'm afraid.'

'How long has he held his present post?'

'Mm, three years? maybe a little bit longer.'

'Have you any specific reason to suspect him, Mrs Wyndham-Brookes?'

'Yes, only it's all so vague I hesitate to tell you. You see, I have thought for some time that there is something sinister or creepy about Mr Stringer. He slinks about the place, nursing his insignificance, and I have never understood how the bishop endured him.'

'And why might he have wished the bishop ill?'

'Because I was urging the bishop to appoint him to a country living so that the bishop could then employ a secretary of stature and distinction who would befit the see of Worcester.'

'And you're suggesting that Mr Stringer got wind of your manoeuvre?'

'Inspector, it was not a "manoeuvre", as you term it. It was my clear duty to protect the bishop from weaklings and encourage him to place his correspondence and his diary in the hands of someone worthier. Yes, the more I think of it, the more certain I am that he is your man, inspector.'

'If he's been with you for three years, can you think of any reason why he should have waited until now to act? It doesn't seem very likely.'

'Well, it's obvious, perfectly obvious, inspector. Yesterday was the feast of St Giles.'

'I'm afraid you'll have to explain a little more fully, Mrs Wyndham-Brookes.'

'Catholics and Anglicans celebrate the feast of St Giles on 1 September.'

'And who was St Giles?' I naturally asked.

'His life and legend are inextricably mixed. Apparently a tenth-century biography has so muddied the waters that hagiographers now have the greatest difficulty in extracting any reliable historical facts at all, so I probably can't give you a very coherent account, but let me tell you this much, which must have a direct bearing on my poor husband's death. St Giles was probably a seventh-century hermit living in the south of France. The story goes that his only companion was a hind. One day, the king and his huntsmen chased the deer to the saint's hermitage and shot at it with an arrow. The arrow hit the saint and not the deer. The king was full of apology and offered the saint medical care and gifts, all of which he refused, but in subsequent months he cultivated the saint's acquaintance as a holy man. Eventually he persuaded the saint to accept the abbotship of a new monastery he built nearby at his own expense, and there St Giles eventually died in an odour of the greatest sanctity.'

'How does this tie in with your husband's death?' was my next and natural question.

'Well, don't you see, inspector, St Giles was offered preferment by the monarch for the good of the Church. The parallel with my husband is obvious. The murderer showed his contempt by killing the bishop just as he was on the edge of great advancement, on the very day when the Church celebrates the virtues of the French hermit.'

I spent a few moments digesting this parallel, which I confess I thought a little fanciful. The little story prompted me to contemplate once again the credulity of the Middle Ages, where almost any story gained credence provided only that it promised the listener some sort of benefit. We can despise such simple faith, but is our own age any better, characterised as it is by belief in astrology and in the power of mascots and talismans, by trust in 'lucky' charms and amulets, by resort to obscure forces supposedly influential in human life, and so on? The advance of science and the spread of education have not weaned people off unsubstantiated, fantastic and far-fetched attitudes. If fate chose to protect the innocent hind at St Giles' expense, I was happy to accept the story as just that.

'Thank you very much, Mrs Wyndham-Brookes,' I said eventually. 'We may well have to see you later, if you don't mind, but you have been very helpful so far. May I repeat how sorry we are to have to be here today?'

Next on our list was the chaplain, Mr David Skyner. I am not a nervous man, and I do not think that I am easily intimidated, but I could understand that some people might be overawed by Mr Skyner's imposing physique and energetic manner. Here was a man not to be disconcerted by the mere death of his employer; I determined on a bold approach.

'Mr Skyner,' I said, 'you had the ear of the bishop. He trusted you and would be advised by you. Did he ever mention an enemy, a fear, a recent threat, perhaps?'

'Inspector, the bishop was a very placid man. Of course, his high churchmanship put some people off, and I daresay that, like every person in the public eye, he was not popular in every quarter, but I can assure you that no overt threat has been made, to my knowledge, well, certainly not recently, probably ever.'

'At the moment, it looks as if the bishop was killed by a member of the household, although I have to say that it does only *look* that way. Would you, as bishop's chaplain and confidant and right-hand man, have any suspicion at all?'

'I'm not sure it's my position to be voicing suspicions about anyone, inspector.'

'Mr Skyner, this is a murder investigation. The sergeant and I are utterly discreet, and we do need people to talk frankly to us. In any case, you are better placed than most to guide us through the intricacies of the bishop's life and career.' I waited for the chaplain's response to this firm and unambiguous plea.

'Well,' he said, 'I suppose you are right: perhaps I did know the bishop better than most, because I certainly made it my business to keep tacks on his acquaintance, partly to protect him from undesirables. On the other hand, there are other people in the household, you know, whose aim was to undermine the bishop.'

When he paused, I prompted him. 'Please go on, sir.'

'Let me not conceal from you, then, inspector, if I *have* to speak, that I have never trusted the almoner. He's a dull, unimaginative fellow. Now let me be quite clear that I say nothing about his official duties: I have no reason to doubt that he carries them out meticulously.'

'But?'

'But I have suspected him for some time of having his eye on Mrs Wyndham-Brookes. I have caught him several times looking at her doe-eyed: really rather nauseating, if the truth be told. If that's the way he feels about her, the honourable course of action, in my opinion, would be to resign and seek a post away from here.'

'Yes, Mr Skyner, but we don't always think so honourably, and in your own estimation Mr Blake lacks imagination. Perhaps he simply doesn't know that his feelings for Mrs Wyndham-Brookes, if that's what they are, are quite so obvious.'

'Maybe not, but who's going to tell him that he's making a fool of himself and should go?'

'I shall leave that for you to decide, sir, but are you telling me that what he feels for his employer's wife might lead him to take the bishop's life?'

'It's not for me to say, inspector, but if I were to point the finger at a member of the Hartlebury household in connection with his lordship's death, as you request, it would be at Mr Blake, I'm afraid. I can't think of anyone else who would have the effrontery to contemplate such a crime.'

'And do you know for a certainty that he was in the castle last night?'

'Yes, I do. He has an office on the premises and keys to enable him to come and go as he wishes. The side entrance used at night by members of the household who do not live at Hartlebury is unobtrusive, and somebody can enter and leave with little chance of being seen. In any case, the secretary, the almoner and the archdeacon all have excellent excuses to be in the castle at any reasonable hour of the day or night. I do hope I have not sowed undeserved suspicion in your mind, inspector.'

'No, no, Mr Skyner,' I assured him, 'we should much prefer plain talking to shilly-shallying and pussyfootery.' (Or should that have been pussyfootage?) 'You can be confident that nothing we hear will be used for any but the most stringently relevant purposes.'

Mr Stringer, the secretary, next on our list, entered, unsmiling and sombre. Since it was unlikely, I thought, that he would be taken on by

Bishop Wyndham-Brookes' successor, he was probably contemplating the uncertainty of his future. That, however, is doubtless integral to the life of a clergyman, except for those fortunate enough to land a permanent living. I had asked Sergeant Hewitt to start our conversation off. Perhaps at the back of my mind was an intention to wrong-foot the secretary. The first case that Hewitt and I worked on together was the Longdon Murders, three and a half years before, and I had been impressed from the start with his sense of humour, sense of fun, willingness to learn and above all reliability. He was a very comfortable companion to be with. Now in his early thirties, he was a Cornishman born and bred, with a charming young wife who worked as a teaching assistant in a school in Stourport, and two daughters now at secondary school.

'Mr Stringer,' said Hewitt, 'may I say how sorry Inspector Wickfield and I are that the bishop has met such an unpleasant end? It cannot be easy for you to talk about it.'

The secretary shook his head in what I interpreted as dejection but pronounced his willingness to talk to us nevertheless.

'Can you conceive of any reason why someone might wish to murder the bishop? You were in his confidence: probably as close to him in his professional life as anyone else, except perhaps his chaplain. Did he ever mention concern over a threat or a danger to his personal safety?'

The secretary did not immediately reply.

'Look, sergeant,' he said at length, 'I want to be helpful, but I don't want to speak out of turn. In any case, I'm still stunned by the turn of events.'

'Take your time, sir. We do need as much help as possible from those close to the bishop, and I can assure you that anything you tell us is completely confidential until such time as the inspector chooses to make an arrest.'

'Well, then, sergeant, I have long suspected Mrs Wyndham-Brookes of becoming impatient with her husband's loss of ambition. You see, they are really quite different in character. The bishop was losing the motivation of his youth: he seemed content to subside into early retirement, perhaps tired of the daily effort to maintain an important job at a time of such upheavals, both in the world and in the Church. His wife, on the other hand, is determined to go higher.'

'May I ask how you can be sure of this?'

'I have on quite a number of occasions, particularly recently, heard her urging her husband to think bigger, to go higher, to aim for the chairmanship of this committee or membership of that body, but he keeps saying that he has enough on his plate already.'

'I see. Thank you. Have you any reason, however, to think that she would take active steps to end her husband's life? Wanting her husband to be more ambitious is still a long way from bringing about his death, you know.'

'It is, of course, sergeant, but I have come to notice an increasingly harsh and ruthless streak in Mrs W-B. The bishop was over sixty and talking about early retirement. She wasn't getting any younger and could see preferment slipping from her grasp. She was increasingly edgy and sharp-tongued. There's another thing, too, although I mention it only in passing. I have noticed that letters were arriving regularly from the bishop's palace in Chichester, addressed to Mrs Wyndham-Brookes, and I thought there might be some sort of intrigue going on. Sheer imagination on my part, I daresay you'll tell me, and you're probably right. I perhaps shouldn't have mentioned it at all, but if it helps in any way to bring this nasty case to a successful conclusion ... ' He trailed off uncertainly but then resumed. 'There's one other thing, sergeant, but you may think it just too fanciful for words.'

'I should be glad to hear it,' Hewitt said indulgently.

'Forgive me if I speak to those already well-informed, but yesterday was the feast of St Giles.'

'Yes, I believe it was,' the sergeant commented guardedly. 'What relevance could that have?'

'Well, there is very little reliable historical evidence about St Giles – St Giles of Saint-Gilles-du-Gard in Provence, the famous one, I'm talking about – and one thing for which he is known in the popular imagination is a lack of ambition. So, for example, according to a later *Life* of him, he was born in Greece but fled that country when his miracles and holiness made him the object of popular veneration. Later, when he had settled in Provence, he lived in solitude deep in the forest, far from any risk of a popular cult. When the king wanted to shower him with favours, after a chance meeting during a hunt, he refused them all, although he was finally persuaded to accept a few disciples. By some he was confused with an earlier bishop of Arles, and this gave him an episcopal status he shunned. All in all, St Giles is the perfect prototype of our dear late bishop, inspector.'

'And so?'

'And so – and here you will have enough experience and wisdom to assess my suggestion as speculation – Mrs W-B struck on the saint's feast day, to express her contempt for her husband's pusillanimity.'

'But surely,' Hewitt insisted, 'St Giles' lack of ambition eventually gained him world renown. Would Mrs W-B not wish that on her husband?'

'Sheer legend, sergeant. The tenth-century *Life* is unbelievably adulatory and designed to further the claims of the town of Saint-Gilles-du-Gard to be a recognised stopping-place on the pilgrimage to Compostella. No, no, you can take it from me that St Giles, the historical personage, was a retiring wannabe hermit who died in obscurity and later had an undeserved miraculous life thrust on him to benefit the local town. I'm sorry, sergeant, I seem to have wandered grossly from my script. You'd probably be best advised to ignore me.'

'No, no, you've been very helpful, Mr Stringer,' I chipped in. 'Perhaps you'd be good enough to tell Mr Blake we should like a word with him.'

THREE

Our next visitor, therefore, was the almoner. The first impression of the Reverend Havelock Blake was not alluring. His feeble frame and nervous deportment made him an unlikely candidate for the bishop's wife's affections – I thought, perhaps uncharitably – but every man has a right to his ideals and to affection in his life; and his present function was undoubtedly important. I wondered about his Christian name – forename, really, because there is no St Havelock that I know of. The authorities that I have read seem to differ on its origin and significance: most derive it from some northern European language: German or a Scandinavian tongue. Some interpret it to mean Sea-Race or Sea-Games; others explain it as a form of Oliver, meaning Elf-Warrior, or possibly Ancestor. Two famous carriers of it were Havelock Ellis, the psychologist, and Havelock Nelson, the composer. Why had Mr Blake's parents chosen a relatively unusual name for their offspring? I mused on. What if I told you that Stan Wickfield is a pseudonym: that my birth name was Bulstrode Lomas, and that I changed it for professional purposes as being easier on the tongue or easier to remember or simply less outlandish? Which would be my 'real' name? We all know Rocinante ('Previously a Nag') as Rocinante: but that was not its 'real' name, which we never discover!

Thrusting these musings aside, I put to Mr Havelock Blake the same question we had asked his predecessors in the inquisitor's chair. He replied with aplomb.

'Inspector, I'm afraid I'm quite the wrong person to ask. You see, I'm not really privy to the ways of the household. I come to see the bishop for particular reasons, and I go just as quietly. My office is isolated, and I work on my own. Of course, I know all the others who work here, but really I've no insight at all into how the castle works in detail.'

'Well, I accept that to some extent, Mr Blake, but I must press you further. You were after all an habitué of the place, you knew everyone, you must have heard things in the course of your duties. The bishop has met an untimely death. We need any help you can give us.'

'I'm not one to gossip, inspector. It is uncharitable to speak ill of others.'

'On the other hand, sir, you have a duty to see that justice prevails, I trust you will agree.'

'Oh, this is so difficult, if you put it like that.'

'I do put it like that, Mr Blake.'

'Then you are asking me to weigh my duties in charity against my duties in justice.'

'You are not being charitable by allowing a person to get away with murder: and it is an act of uncharity against the victim.'

'It is, inspector. I see you've been brushing up on your moral theology.' He said this without a trace of humour. 'The only thing I can say in reply – and I repeat that I speak to some extent under compulsion - is that the bishop had discussed with me the housekeeper's position.'

Since he stopped speaking at this point, I urged him on.

'The bishop told me that his wife had complained about Mrs Wedlake and wanted her replaced.'

'I don't quite see how that comes within your remit, sir.'

'Well, inspector, the bishop was worried about Mrs Wedlake's future: how would she survive? He wondered whether she might be a case for special consideration, and that's why he asked for my opinion.'

'And how would murdering the bishop help the housekeeper? Would it not have been better to murder the bishop's wife? I ask only as a matter of abstract theory.'

'The bishop's wife, inspector: Mrs Wyndham-Brookes? Have you taken leave of your senses? Why would anyone in their right mind contemplate murdering such a fine woman?'

'But I don't see how murdering the bishop would help Mrs Wedlake's situation.'

'Inspector, let me explain. Mrs Wyndham-Brookes, as I understand the matter, had given Mrs Wedlake the impression that it was the bishop who had lodged the complaint with her, the bishops' wife. She felt, in her kindness, that this would soften the blow for Mrs Wedlake: this was not just

24

some minor conflict of interest between two women, which the housekeeper could resent, but, so to speak, a matter of state, with a decision taken at the highest level. Mrs Wyndham-Brookes wanted Mrs Wedlake to understand that the smooth running of the castle was more important than the position of one employee. Mrs Wedlake was being sacrificed for the good of the whole, and in any case her financial future would not be neglected.'

'I see,' I commented, although I was not sure I quite did. 'Would Mrs Wedlake be capable of murder, do you think, Mr Blake? That's quite a step to take, you know.'

'Of course, Mrs Wyndham-Brookes could not foresee that the housekeeper would take the news quite so badly. The pill had been sufficiently sugared, but what she did not quite understand – and I got this from the bishop in the course of the conversation I mentioned earlier – was that the castle was not just employment to Mrs Wedlake: it was her life. In her desperation, she might, I surmise, have thought of the ultimate sanction.'

I wondered whether the almoner was protecting Mrs W-B. I put to myself a contrary case. Mrs Wedlake knew full well that the bishop's wife was behind any move to oust her; she would punish her where it would most hurt: by destroying any prospect of advancement in the person of her husband. We had not yet met Mrs Wedlake, so I was not in a position to assess her likelihood as a murderess. It would not be long before she was sitting before us.

The buxom Mrs Wedlake was everything one would expect in a housekeeper: a bustling type, large in the upper arm, broad in the leg, heavy of feature. Her face was serious, but I could imagine it, in happier circumstances, brightly suffused with cheerfulness. Traces of tears – but whether of grief or joy, or perhaps just raw emotion at the unexpected turn of events, I could not judge - stained her face. I again invited Sergeant Hewitt to conduct the interview. He was confident in the execution of this difficult duty – owing in great part, I have no doubt, to my careful coaching over the years! - and his keen young face and courteous manner eased his interviewees, particularly the women, into appropriate moods of self-revelation.

'Mrs Wedlake,' he began, 'we appreciate your readiness to speak to us at this terrible time.' She nodded. 'Do you think you could answer one or two questions for us?' She gave another nod. 'Good, thank you. Can you think of any reason why anyone should wish to harm his lordship?'

'I'm not given to gossip, sergeant. It's not for me to say.'

Hewitt followed my lead (although his remarks perhaps sprang spontaneously to his lips) in insisting on the housekeeper's duty to help us in the cause of justice, and, after his short but eloquent speech, Mrs Wedlake surrendered.

'I had occasion recently,' she said, 'to suspect the archdeacon of manoeuvrings against the bishop.'

'Manoeuvrings against the bishop?' Hewitt queried, with a touch of disbelief in his tone, which I hope Mrs Wedlake did not notice.

'Look, sergeant,' Mrs Wedlake said, 'I don't understand these things very well, but I shall explain as best I can. I've picked up quite a bit during my time here. Our Church is an uneasy coexistence of two opposing schools, evangelicalism and catholicism, and although most people manage to coexist quite happily, there are bitter feelings at the extremities. Now his lordship, as I understand the matter, was Anglo-Catholic, while the archdeacon was somewhere in the middle – until recently, when he became a rabid evangelical. That's when he began to harbour hostile thoughts against his lordship.' She sat back. Evidently the same thought occurred to Hewitt as it did to me, because he told her admiringly that she seemed well-informed on the subject (*in pectore*, for a housekeeper!).

'Well,' she said with a slight blush, 'Mr Blake does me the kindness of dropping in to the kitchen or the sewing-room for his cups of tea, since he hasn't a sink in his office, and, well, you know, we chat, about this and that – well, you know how it is, sergeant.'

'Yes, indeed, Mrs Wedlake, I quite understand; and was it Mr Blake who mentioned the almoner's change of heart?'

'It was. Apparently Mr Rolfe made no secret of it: "fidelity to the Word of the Lord compels me," he said, "to draw the world's attention to the bishop's errors". That's what Mr Blake reported to me.'

'And did Mr Blake tell you what form the "manoeuvrings" might take?'

'No, only that Mr Rolfe was stirring things up amongst the canons, the deans and other clergy against the bishop, claiming that he was leading the diocese astray and should be replaced at the first opportunity – by which I took him to mean the bishop's retirement. Oh, dear, sergeant, I daresay you'll think I'm out of my depth in all these matters. You're right, of course, but I'm only telling you what Mr Blake told me: I can't really judge for myself.'

'Mrs Wedlake,' Hewitt pursued inexorably, 'had you any reason to think that your own employment at the castle was at risk?'

'Yes, that Mrs Wyndham-Brookes woman took it on herself to express the bishop's dissatisfaction with my work, but I reckon it's her that wants me out. Well, she can whistle. They can't get rid of me that easily. I've got rights, you know.'

'What would you do if you ever had to leave the castle?'

'I don't know.' She blushed again, deeply. 'My dream,' she said with matronly bashfulness, 'would be to remarry and move into my husband's vicarage – I mean, house. That would be wonderful. If nothing came of that, in God's providence, I should have to look for a new situation, I suppose, and I know I should not enjoy it half so much as I do life here, so it would be very difficult for me.'

'How do you think your present position might change in the event of a change of bishop, Mrs Wedlake? Do incoming bishops bring their own housekeeper with them?'

'If they have any sense, they take over existing staff, that's my view: people who know the place and its quirks. That's what happened when the present bishop moved in: I'd been here for years already; but of course they don't take on their predecessor's wife, so that Wyndham-Brookes woman will be gone, that'd be one gain.'

'May I ask how long you have worked here, Mrs Wedlake?'

'Fifteen years, ever since my husband died. Up till then I'd worked in the retail trade, but we had a tied cottage, you see, because of my husband's job, and I was given three months to move out when Sam passed on. I saw this advertisement for a housekeeper, and I thought I could do the job as well as the next woman, so I applied: and here I am!'

The morning was now wearing on, and we had yet to interview the archdeacon. The housekeeper was asked to convey our desire to have a few words with the archdeacon, if he was on the premises and could spare us the time. That was a polite way of indicating our summons. In view of the night's events, the archdeacon was certainly on the premises, if only to help organise interim measures of running the diocese, summoned earlier, no doubt, by the efficient Mr Stringer. Of all our interviewees so far, Mr Rolfe most closely fitted my identikit picture of a murderer, with his pasty skin and jutting teeth and permanent scowl, but I have to admit that his manner was irreproachable; and here, unmistakeably, was an earnest man. (Do you recall Lady Clarinda's description of Mr Crotchet *fils* in Peacock's *Crotchet Castle?* 'He looks,' she says, 'as if he had tumbled headlong into a volcano and been thrown up again among the cinders.' That would certainly fit the archdeacon of Worcester!)

'As you are no doubt well aware, Mr Rolfe,' I began, 'we are investigating his lordship's most unfortunate death during the night. You were on the premises?'

'No, not really, inspector. It is true that I had some work to do, but I left quite soon after tea – about seven, I should think.'

'I see. Now did the bishop mention to you, in the last weeks or months, any cause for fear or anxiety? any threat to his life?'

'No, nothing, inspector, nothing at all. His lordship was invariably calm and equable, a pleasure to work for.'

'Please take my next question in the spirit of inquiry in which it is meant, Mr Rolfe. You were appointed archdeacon by his late lordship.'

'I was.'

'You were familiar with those closest to his lordship.'

'Yes, I suppose you could say that.'

'Have you any suspicion what could lie behind his death?'

The archdeacon did not reply at once.

'Inspector,' he said eventually, 'we live in difficult times. There is such ferment in the Church, it is no wonder people are unsettled, but there you are. You may know – of course you will if you're an Anglican – that evangelicals and catholics in the Church don't exactly get on and each side wishes to see its own partisans in positions of high office. At the moment, the bishop has at his right hand a learned and undoubtedly capable man who happens to be a high churchman of unimpeachable credentials. If I speak against this man in the present forum, inspector, I shouldn't wish you to suppose that I do so out of pique. I know that you will be utterly discreet. I shall not disguise from you that I have recently undergone a change of heart. I now see quite clearly that true Anglicanism resides not in the aping of popery, but in adherence to the simple norms of Jesus' gospel. You could say, if you wish to use clumsy categories, that from being broad Church I have become evangelical.

'Whatever words we use, I trust that I can, in consequence of my – yes, let us call it "conversion" - visualise the Church's problems in a clearer light, and I have come to regard the chaplain's ambitions as highly dangerous for the Church. I repeat, inspector: I speak not out of resentment but out of a zealous love of my Church. You may not know that the chaplain also functions as vicar general: not a usual combination of posts, but it has a certain logic. With the bishop removed from the scene, the chaplain would automatically step in to fill his shoes, and he could find himself running the diocese for a considerable time, almost certainly some months. What better springboard from which to grasp at a bishopric of his own?'

'Pardon me, sir, what evidence have you for the chaplain's ambitions in this direction?'

'Inspector, it is common knowledge amongst those close to the bishop. Mr Skyner's ambition is plain for all to see. Of course, ambition is, in its way, laudable: humankind would never have advanced very far if individuals had not taken vigorous steps to better themselves and their fellows. However, ambition for personal aggrandisement is diabolical in its destructive effects. Does the Psalmist not tell us that "Men who aspire to high degree are altogether lighter than vanity"? And does St Paul not enjoin on us, "Mind not high things"?'

'Tell me, Mr Rolfe, do you really think that this – this "learned and capable" person, as you admit him to be, is capable of murder?'

'Who can tell of what a person is capable, until the circumstances present themselves? A circumstance like the present one may never come his way again.'

'What have you in mind, exactly? Do you know of any reason why your "suspect" should move at precisely this time?'

'Yes, I do, but it would take a little time to explain, inspector.'

'Please give us some idea, as we need to understand.'

'Well, earlier this year, in March it was, I can't remember the exact date, the Archbishop of Canterbury was received by the pope in the Vatican – that was the first time there had been such an official meeting in 400 years of what the Catholics call schism - we prefer to say separation. It was stated at the time that a joint working-party would be set up to try to remove the obstacles that still separated Anglicanism from Roman Catholicism. Preparatory to that working-party – talks about talks - some theologians from both sides were going to meet here in England to draw up an outline agenda, and his lordship was keen to take part. In the event he was nominated chairman of this opening meeting, at which seven areas of debate were identified, and various people were asked to prepare papers in these areas as grounds for discussion. If the bishop should die in harness, so to speak, his successor might well be asked to take his place as chairman of the committee, if only temporarily. I suppose there might be a wider consideration here: no room must be given to the possibility that the talks might falter through lack of momentum, and his late lordship's flagging energies might be taken as a threat.'

'I see,' I said in reply. 'That might be very helpful.'

'There is something else, inspector, which I am prompted to tell you by the odd coincidence, if that is what it was, of the timing of the bishop's death. It may be quite irrelevant, but I know you will quickly sift it out if the information is of no use to you.'

'Thank you for that note of confidence. Please continue.'

'Yesterday was the feast of St Giles, and of course, as you know, the bishop's Christian name was Giles. Now St Giles is surrounded by legend. One of these legends relates that he was once standing on the sea-shore when he saw a boat in difficulties in a storm. He prayed fervently to God, the storm ceased at once, and the sailors made it safely to shore. In answer to his question, they informed him that they were on their way to Rome, and he begged leave to join them. They gladly received him on board, set sail once again and refused to accept his offer of payment for his passage.'

I wondered idly how this medieval legend would now be applied to the Bishop of Worcester's death, although, in view of the almoner's previous disclosures, I could guess more or less what was coming!

'So you see, inspector, this all ties in with what I was saying earlier. St Giles was making his way to Rome with a free and easy passage. In the event he never got there, at least not on that occasion, because he stopped off at Arles and ended up spending some years there as a hermit. Our murderer is stepping in to prevent Providence from repeating such a mistake. The bishop was moving the Anglican Church to Rome, but lacked heart; his aims had to be advanced willy-nilly. Even if he himself was allowed to slink away to a hermitage in remote Provençal countryside, the voyage must continue! Now to you and me this may seem a somewhat drastic step, but, you know, where the perceived truth of the gospel is at stake ... Well, there you are.'

'If what you say has any legitimacy, you too have every excuse for wishing to see the bishop removed, as a threat to the present character of the Church.'

'Yes, but not through murder, inspector. Heaven help us, what a thought! No, I was quite content to await the bishop's translation, or retirement or – natural death, whichever should come first. Everything will come in God's good time; and then we shall have an evangelical at the reins of power!'

I pride myself that these initial interviews had been decorously and effectively conducted. We had gleaned much information; quite how reliable it all was was another matter. I asked Hewitt just to draw up a table with our main findings – to concentrate the mind. What he came up with is shown in the table on the next page.

I then invited him to make appropriate comments.

'Well, sir,' he said, 'I have to admit that I have quite enjoyed myself so far. This is a new world to me, and it's been an interesting experience.'

'Please stick to the facts, sergeant: hard, tough, immutable, undeniable facts.'

'Yessir, of course, sir. Well, one undoubted fact is that we can't trust anything we've been told: these people are a bunch of self-seeking, time-serving, narrow-minded, blinkered, insular inmates of a claustrophobic institution – '

'I must stop you there, sergeant, and correct your initial impressions. These people, as you dismissively call them, have an important job to do, and we must credit them all with the sincerity and open vision and strength of purpose that their roles require, until shown incontrovertibly otherwise.

name	position ⟶	suspect	alleged motive
Mrs Sybil Wyndham-Brookes	deceased's wife	Revd Stringer	he feared that the bishop was about to dismiss him from his post for being weak and inadequate (or have him defrocked)
Revd Mr David Skyner	chaplain	Revd Blake	Blake, having amorous designs on Mrs W-B, wanted the bishop removed
Revd Mr Simon Stringer	secretary	Mrs W-B	she deplored her husband's lack of ambition and desired marriage with someone more motivated, viz the bishop of Colchester
Revd Mr Havelock Blake	almoner	Mrs Wedlake	the threat to her job, which was her life, came from the bishop, and she determined to retaliate
Mrs Myrtle Wedlake	housekeeper	Mr Rolfe	he wanted an evangelical to occupy the see of Worcester
Ven Mr Maddock Rolfe	archdeacon	Mr Skyner	he wished to step into the bishop's shoes so as to be able to foster the Church's move to Rome

Even if there is a murderer amongst them, it is probably only one of them: that leaves the other five leading blameless and holy lives in the service of a venerable and august body. So, please start again.'

Hewitt, suitably chastened (I hoped), took a breath and began again.

'Right, sir. Let us start with the hypothesis that one of them is responsible for the bishop's death. It is naturally in his or her interest to deflect our attention by naming someone else as the murderer. This they could do without arousing suspicion, because we impressed on them the need to assist the processes of justice. Let us now ask ourselves why the other five – whoever they are – also named a suspect. There might be a number of motives for this, but two immediately spring to mind without necessarily arousing our distaste. One is that we have urged them to help us in speaking out: they would all naturally wish to be seen to be assisting us in our inquiries. The second is that they genuinely wish to protect the bishop or the Church or the other employees from an undeserving fellow-traveller. Of course, they could also be taking the opportunity to settle old scores, but you've told me to discount that as a motive – sir!'

'Do you think that we have any reliable information at all amongst the dross?'

'Yes, sir, I do. I think we can rely on statements of fact, although we need to discount them as motives for murder.'

'Go on.'

'OK, let's take as an example the sorrowing widow. She came across, to me at any rate, as an insufferably self-satisfied woman with a higher status in her sights. Mr Stringer's remarks therefore make sense: the bishop and his wife were quite different in character, he had lost his motivation, she was anxious to climb higher, she had, in Stringer's hearing, several times urged her husband to think about applying for positions of influence, and so on. His understanding of the situation is probably sensible and accurate. That Mrs W-B's feelings were the basis of murder is quite another matter, and we should probably be very wise – like you, sir – to exclude the chaplain's suspicions.'

'Fine,' I said graciously, basking in the warmth of Hewitt's unsolicited testimonial.

'Or take the housekeeper. According to Mr Blake, who is obviously unaware of, or perhaps indifferent to, Mrs Wedlake's partiality towards him, the housekeeper is told by Mrs Wyndham-Brookes that the bishop intends to replace her. She can't bear the thought of being dismissed from the castle, where she has lived and worked for the last fifteen years. We can surely take that much as the truth. When, however, the almoner goes on to suggest that her fear has translated itself into murder of the bishop, we suspend our belief. That's how I see things, anyway, sir.'

'Yes, sergeant, thank you for that. I probably agree with what you say, but what struck me most forcefully is that, if the bishop's own household is riven by rivalry and intrigue, what hope is there for the wider Church?'

FOUR

The reader now has every right to an apology: I have completely forgotten to tell you, so keen was I to introduce to you the main *dramatis personae,* about the discovery of the crime! Let me repair this lapse at once. This was the way of it.

It was the secretary's wont to arrive at the castle at eight o'clock in the morning, let himself in by the side-door with his own key, make his way to his lordship's study and begin the day by sorting out the appointments and, at about half-past eight or thereabouts, after the visit of the postman's van, start going through the morning's mail. On this particular morning – Friday 2 September – he followed his usual routine, but when, having traversed the great hall and the salon, he reached the bishop's study, he was surprised to find it locked on the inside: he could see the end of the key in the lock. This was so unusual - indeed, in his experience unique – that he was unaccustomedly nonplussed. He knocked loudly, several times, but his summons remained unanswered. He made his way back outside, noticing that the front-door was properly locked, in order to peer in through one of the windows, but the curtains were drawn. He hurried back inside and tried to gain entry through the annexe that intervened between the chapel and the study, but that door too was locked. He decided that his proper course of action was to call the police, even before rousing the household. Hence our early visit to Hartlebury Castle on that memorable September morning.

The secretary, having greeted us at the front-door, conducted us into the hall and taken us through his exact movements that morning – having, in short, exhausted his reserves of ready assistance - left the next move to us. My first action was to ask where we might find another key to the main study door. We were told that both keys habitually hung on a hook inside the study door. Having checked that no more reasonable entry could be gained either at the window or at the annexe door, I ordered the lock on the annexe door of the study to be broken with a hammer: I had my suspicions already, you see, as I shall relate in the appropriate place.

The scene that greeted us – Hewitt, Stringer and myself, plus Mrs Wyndham-Brookes, the chaplain and the housekeeper, who had all by this time joined us – was not designed to lift the spirits. The first object to catch the eye was his lordship's body, hunched on the hearth-rug with the head lying in the hearth surrounded by a pool of blood. We next took in the ruck in the hearth-rug, where the bishop had caught his foot and tripped, before knocking his head on the fender. The fire had burnt itself out. The ceiling-lights were on, as was a reading lamp on the desk. The curtains, as you know, were drawn, but I drew them back the better to clarify the scene and to render it less macabre. Having asked the chaplain to telephone for a murder-scene squad and for a vehicle to remove the body, I asked the members of the household to withdraw so that Hewitt and I could make a proper survey of the scene. Before they left the room, however, the chaplain drew our attention to a curious circumstance.

'Inspector,' he said, 'I notice that his lordship had our incunabulum on his desk.'

'Yes,' I answered non-committally, not at first seeing the relevance of the point.

'It is the library's only incunabulum, a 1476 copy of Jacobus de Voragine's *Legenda Aurea*.' I should perhaps add at this point, probably unnecessarily, erudite reader, that Jacobus is, if we imitate the chaplain, pronounced with the stress on the middle syllable. Hewitt and I went over to the desk to look and asked the chaplain to explain what we were looking at.

'Jacobus de Voragine was a Dominican friar, born in about 1230. In his early sixties, he was consecrated bishop of his native city of Genoa, and there he died six or seven years later. His two most famous writings are a history of Genoa and this *Legenda Aurea*, although he was also responsible for much else, including volumes of sermons and a work on the Virgin Mary. The *Legenda Aurea*, compiled in about 1260, is a collection of saints' lives in which the fanciful and the fantastic have pride of place. We are very pleased to have a copy in the castle library. You see, it was probably the most famous book of its kind for centuries, extremely widely read and very influential.'

'I see,' I commented. 'And what is its significance here?'

'Two things, inspector. Firstly, the book is marked at the life of St Giles, as you can see if I open the book a trace, 1 September, yesterday's date; and secondly, the book is in Middle French and Gothic script.'

'Yes, yes,' I said, a touch sharply. 'What of it?'

'Well,' the chaplain said, 'the bishop couldn't read Middle French: Greek, yes, Latin, yes, modern French a little, but not Middle French!'

If the chaplain had never told us that, I doubt whether we should ever have solved the mystery of the bishop's death. I chewed over the information for a few moments.

When we were alone, Hewitt asked me at once why I had not taken the scene at face value as a sad accident. His reading was that the bishop had approached the fire, perhaps to warm his hands on a cool evening, caught his foot in the rug, pitched forward and struck his head fatally on the metal fender. There he had lain until the secretary's ineffective attempt at entry that morning.

'Well,' I said cautiously, 'the secretary had already alerted us to the possibility of foul play by remarking that the bishop had never before been known to lock his door. When I peered through the key-hole from the salon, I noticed that the teeth of the key were vertical, placed in such a way, therefore, that the key could be slid out, if the person locking the door on the inside were so minded, without its needing to be turned.'

'I'm sorry, sir, I don't see what bearing that point could have on anything.'

'Think back to the last time you locked a door and left the key in the lock. I bet you left it so that the teeth were in contact with the plate; you would not have turned the key back to the vertical position, as if with a view to withdrawing it.'

'So?'

'My conclusion is that the key was put in the lock from the outside of the door, and then, in his hurry, the operator forgot to twist it out of perpendicular, which he could have done, with every appearance of verisimilitude, if he had thought about it.'

'I'm sorry, sir: could you please explain that more carefully? You seem to be making a great deal of what is a tiny detail.'

'OK,' I said patiently, 'let's go right back to 1935. This'll be good for your general education, apart from anything else! In 1935, the crime fiction writer

John Dickson Carr, or Carter Dickson, as he sometimes called himself, wrote a book called *The Hollow Man* which includes a famous lecture by the principal – and amateur - investigator, Dr Gideon Fell. Now I confess that in my view the lecture is neither well-structured nor particularly clear, but I think we can use some of the doctor's thoughts to construct a little lesson of our own. Chapter 17 of the book is titled "The Locked-Room Lecture", and it professedly applies to detective fiction, not to real-life crimes. A so-called locked-room mystery – although as I shall point out, that is something of a misnomer - is one in which a person is found dead with every appearance of having been murdered but without obvious evidence of how the murderer entered or left the room. The windows are shut and locked, the door or doors are shut and locked, the victim's body is alone in the room. Now we can identify nine plausible ways – I am reorganising Fell's lecture-notes - in which this might be accomplished. Let me take you through them rapidly, sergeant, one by one.

1. there is a secret passage through which the murderer effects his egress, or he escapes up the chimney. This, according to Fell, is a foul!

2. the murder weapon is introduced into the room through an aperture. For example, a knife is dropped through a hole in the ceiling, a hand is poked through a swinging panel, poisonous gas is pumped into the room, a venomous snake is introduced through a conduit, as in a famous Sherlock Holmes case. This also, according to Dr Fell, is a foul, although quite why I am not sure!

3. the murder is a misunderstanding: in fact the victim meets his death through accident.

4. the victim is driven to suicide, for example, by a haunting, or by a gas which makes him lose his reason.

5. the victim commits suicide but dresses it up as murder in order to implicate another person.

6. the murder is committed by means of a mechanical device concealed in the room, which the victim opens, or bumps into, or lifts, or sits on, etc.

7. the victim is presumed dead long before he actually is: he is killed by the first one to enter the room.

8. the murderer locks the door from the outside, but because he is the first to re-enter the locked room, he is able, surreptitiously of course, to insert the key on the inside as if it had been there all along.

9. the murderer tampers with the door or the window to make it look as if they were locked by the room's sole inmate before he met his death.

Now other writers have worked on this list,' I continued. 'I could mention the pseudonymous American magician and novelist Clayton Rawson, who had a go in his – or perhaps I should more correctly say 'their' - first book, *Death from a Top Hat* of 1938, I think it was. He/they reduced all locked-room mysteries to three categories, which is so logically simple as to have a certain superficial appeal: 1. the killer contrives the murder from outside the sealed room; 2. the killer kills in the room but tampers with the windows or doors as s/he exits to give the impression that he or she was never there; and 3. the killer is in the room but leaves before the room is thoroughly searched. Anthony Boucher in his crime fiction novel, *Nine Times Nine,* had another go at categorisation two or three years later. In the '50s we could mention Derek Smith's *Whistle Up the Devil.* The solution there is ingenious but quite simple, but I believe the author makes two mistakes. The first is that he claims that a man found with a dagger between his shoulder blades, as is the case in his own work, could not be a suicide; this is not true. The second is that, when discussing ways of locking and unlocking a door from the outside, he does not consider my own little solution with a piece of bent wire! There is also a work, only I forget its exact title and its author – a Frenchman, somebody Lacourbe? - which lists the ninety-nine best closed-room murder books – presumably out of hundreds; but in fact there's a whole industry devoted to the genre. Georges Simenon famously turned his back on it as impractical and improbable.

'Now writers do not always make desirable distinctions, in my opinion. There seems to me no point in setting up a so-called locked-room mystery if the death can be the result only of murder – except that I shall return to that point in a minute. The clever murderer does not want a murder hunt; he wants to disguise the death as suicide or accident, so that his own position is the safer. However secure the room, if the body is, for example, dismembered, or strangled with its hands tied behind its back, the detective, however dim-witted - '

'Why are you looking at me, sir?'

' - is unlikely to come to a conclusion of accident or suicide, and he is going to engage the forces of the law in a hunt for the perpetrator. True locked-room deaths, therefore, should ideally fulfil the following criteria: the death should look like accident or suicide; the death is in fact, almost by definition, murder; there should be nothing peculiar in itself in the locking of the room or in the state of the body; in the case of suicide, some indication should be given of an intention to kill oneself; in the case of accident, the victim is to look as if he were attending to his normal affairs when the misfortune supervened; the scene should deceive the police and so be ascribed to accident.

'Occasionally, I suppose, the murderer wishes to make it clear, probably to all and sundry, that the death is murder; or perhaps he cannot avoid leaving behind him a murder scene. In which case why does he go to the trouble of setting up a locked-room mystery: why not just leave the scene as obviously that of a murder, with clear methods of execution and escape? To display his ingenuity? Possibly, but too great a risk, in my opinion, in case he makes a mistake. To baffle the police? Again, possibly – except that, in detective fiction, at any rate, he never gets away with it! The reason for this is that the death can be only apparently impossible: in real life – so to speak - there has to be a way in which the scene was set up, and the insightful detective will always rumble it in the end – if he concludes that it really is a case of murder. By mistake, therefore? Hardly! No, the only answer is that he does so to challenge the *reader!* The mystery resides in two possible elements, which may overlap: how the murder was committed; how the murderer escaped. If the police come to the conclusion that the death was accidental, there is no mystery! Locked-room mysteries therefore occur only in literature, because they are deeply unrealistic!

'Let us return to our present case. The position of the key in the main study door, which opens from the salon, is a clear indication that we have to do with the last method named above in our list of nine – although on its own, without the supporting evidence of the Jacobus, I might think twice about coming to such a firm conclusion. How did the murderer achieve the appearance of a room locked on the inside, with the key vertical in the lock? Allow me, sergeant, to speculate, on the basis of little experiments of mine conducted in a misspent youth. In my view, traditional methods using a pair of pliers to tweak the key already in the lock or a piece of string passed under the door just do not work: they are a fiction of detective-story writers. So our murderer has prepared a length of thin but strong wire: I found that wire $1/20^{th}$ of an inch thick is suitable for keys weighing up to 2 ounces, and it is probably best to cut about 15 inches of it, for ease of manipulation. Now at one end – the business end, you might say – he creates a pattern of four U-bends, one after the other, the second and fourth being inverted U's. At this stage it would look a bit like an elaborate Loch Ness monster:

He now bends the first and third U's away from him so that they are at right angles to the second and fourth, and viewed from above, the wire would now look something like this:

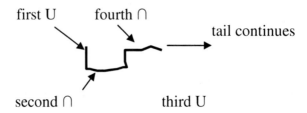

He slots the head of the key (the head on his left, the teeth facing down on the right) into the trough or basin formed by the first and third U's and bends the second U away from him so that it goes into the hole in the head of the key and comes to rest on the upper lip on the far side. He tightens the grip of the wire on the key with a pair of pliers. The point of leaving the main wire branching off horizontally from the *bottom* of the fourth (inverted) U is to keep the teeth of the key balanced just above it so that the wire runs along the bottom of the keyhole while the point of the key is poised to enter the top of the keyhole. So he has this:

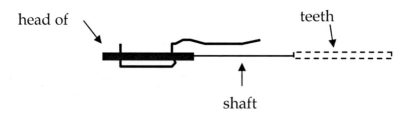

'Now to locking the door! It is, let us say, the dead of night. An owl hoots in the distance; an autumn wind audibly rustles the trees; but the house itself is deadly quiet: there is little chance of the killer's being disturbed, but he is ever so slightly on edge after a murder. He has, however, rehearsed his work. He pokes his wire through the keyhole - with the key on the inside, of course. He leaves the room, closes the door, and with his own key he locks the door, hoping that there is just room for the key to turn unhindered despite the wire running along the bottom of the keyhole. I shall return to this point. He withdraws his key. Now, peering through the keyhole and using the light from the inside of the room, which he has left on to give the impression of an unfortunate accident to the room's occupant, engaged in his lawful business, he manoeuvres his wire until the point of the key, waving in mid-air on the end of his wire, penetrates the keyhole on the far side of the door. He gently pulls the wire towards him, and the key follows its point. When the key is fully in the keyhole, he pulls the wire firmly, and it comes away in his hand. He strides off with a satisfied smirk on his face, pocketing the wire and making for the exit.

'The whole thing requires a bit of research, as my own experiments testified. The wire has to be both sturdy enough to support the weight of the key in question, hanging in space, and yet malleable enough to respond to a jerk which will free the U-bends from the handle and straighten up sufficiently to allow itself to be withdrawn from the lock from the outside. What I intend to convey to you by these remarks is that a criminal is not going to hit on this method by chance or first time: it requires a bit of practice. Let me ask you, young sergeant, without boastfulness, how many people would have spotted the murderer's mistake in this case?'

'And by "mistake", sir, you mean leaving the key vertical in the lock?'

'I do. You see, if he's done as I've described, the wire is stiff enough for him to turn the key before he pulls the wire out; its position round the handle is in any case designed partly to enable him to do so. In his haste he forgot: a bad mistake.'

'Very few would have spotted that, sir: probably, in fact, only yourself!'

'Yes, well, thank you, sergeant. His other mistake was, of course, to lock the room in the first place, as the secretary pointed out.'

'You were going to say something more about the wire in the lock.'

'Yes, I was. You see, this ties in with the other question that must arise in our minds: does the whole scene not indicate a member of the household? Who else could have had access to the key to make a copy? Who else could have investigated the lock first? However, I don't think our reconstruction necessarily implicates a member of the household. Imagine an outsider planning to murder the bishop. If he wishes to leave an accident-scene behind him, he needs to leave the door locked on the inside: that seems fairly clear. What previous information does he need? 1. He needs to know the kind of lock involved: a cylinder lock, for example, won't work. 2. He needs a key. If the key is too heavy, the trick probably won't work either, because he would need a piece of wire too heavy to pull it off the key at the end of his operation. 3. Ideally, he needs to know that there is room in the keyhole for the key and a thin piece of wire. Since the only ways to gain that piece of information are to measure or experiment, he might have preferred to leave it to chance. Older locks generally have a bit of give. A single visit to the bishop's study is sufficient to furnish him with his first two items of information. He sees where the two keys hang and purloins one, hoping the bishop will not notice, or takes a quick cast. One look at the lock will tell him whether it is suitable for his purposes. So much for that. If, in the event, he finds he cannot do as we have described, he simply abandons his plan: unfortunate, but perhaps not disastrous. Now let's look at our other evidence.'

The incunabulum on the desk was marked at folio 236, the beginning of the life of Saint-Gilles. We knew better than to handle so rare a book, but we could see that it was a leather-bound volume of vellum folios, approximately 14 ins x 9 ins and something like 300 pages long, judging by the position of folio 236. Each folio was divided into two columns, significant paragraphs being introduced by a more elaborate first letter in red. We learnt more about the book later, but I shall not trouble you with further information, except for a word about the contents. (The French is much given to abbreviations, and the script, being mediaeval, is difficult to read for one unpractised in the art – certainly beyond me except with a lot of effort. I shall give you a short extract further on, so that you can try for yourself.) The chapter on St Giles, which extends to little more than four columns, begins with a fanciful derivation of his name (= one who is free of earthly concerns and enlightened by the divine love; authorities differ, however, on the real significance: I have read shield, shield-bearer, servant, goat-skin and kid, depending on the supposed language of derivation!) and proceeds with the saint's supposed birth in Athens and three miracles performed in childhood (the cure of a cripple, ridding a snake of all its venom and an exorcism). Then come the story of the sea-voyage towards Rome, related to us later by the secretary, and a further miracle (the cure of a man suffering from a fever for three years).

The saint retires to a desert place and lives as a hermit, bringing fertility and abundance to the land. Popular adulation leads him to retire even further into the desert, where a well and a hind, both provided by God, enable him to survive. The life continues with the story of how the hind is saved from the archers, with which the late bishop's wife regaled us at our first interview with her. The king, mightily impressed, pesters the saint to take charge of a monastery to be built near his hermitage, and finally Giles agrees. The king comes often to see the saint and to confess to him, but he conceals from the saint one sin of which he is particularly ashamed. This sin is not named in the *Legenda Aurea,* but later commentators apparently suggest incest with his sister. Be that as it may, the sin is miraculously identified on a piece of paper laid by an angel on the altar at which the saint is saying Mass. When taxed with it, the king confesses and is forgiven.

Informed of attempts by enemies of the faith to destroy his monastery, Giles sets out for Rome to petition for increased privileges. At Nîmes, he raises a prince's son from the dead. He reaches Rome, where the pope makes him a gift of two doors of cypress, which Giles promptly throws into the Tiber, confident that God will carry them to his monastery (which naturally he does). In due course the saint dies in an odour of sanctity, and many witnesses testify that they heard a company of angels carrying his soul to heaven. According to Jacobus and his sources, Giles flourished around the year 700. Does this story speak to you, gentle reader? I am not sure that many would be impressed by it today, but if you are, I am not one to deny you your belief. (On the other hand, perhaps you should consider the fact that there are seemingly two bodies of St Giles, one in Toulouse and one at Saint-Gilles-du-Gard. Perhaps one was that of the saint as a youth and the other that of the saint in old age!)

FIVE

At the conclusion of the discussion between us following our initial interviews, Hewitt asked me why I had forbidden all mention of the Jacobus volume while we were questioning the members of the episcopal household.

'There are two reasons, sergeant. The first is that I am still thinking my way towards the full significance of the find. The second is that, while I am sure it is a clue, I was unwilling to reveal to our row of "suspects" that we had spotted it - or rather, had it pointed out to us. As you know, a cardinal rule of police interviews is to reveal as little of your hand as possible.'

'And what conclusion have you come to, sir, if I may ask?'

'Tentatively this. If the bishop was not reading the book, somebody else was. How many of the bishop's household read Middle French, and in mediaeval script to boot? The chaplain possibly, and probably no one else, that's my guess. If Mr Skyner is our mystery reader, however, he is certainly bold to point the book out to us. On the whole I incline to the opinion that he is quite innocent in this regard, which means that the bishop was entertaining a visitor last night – or perhaps yesterday – who is not of the household. This – together with the key in the lock - could be the clue we have been looking for.'

'And what reason could there be for the volume to be on the bishop's desk?'

'Well, your suggestions for this, once you bend your great mind to the matter, sergeant, are no doubt as valid as mine. Let us imagine the scene. The bishop's visitor has been let into the building and invited to join the bishop in his study. We cannot tell at this moment whether the meeting was by prior arrangement or unforeseen. We also cannot tell whether the visit

44

was meant to be kept secret or just happened to go unremarked as the day drew to its close and fewer people were about. The bishop and his visitor engage in casual conversation, enjoying the glow of a live fire in the grate, the tranquillity of a rural castle, the comfort of a time-hallowed room. Anyway, the visitor asks to see the library's prize possession, or the bishop offers to show it to him. The motive could be any one of dozens: his lordship wanted the book valued with a view to a sale; he was so proud of it that he wished to show it off; the visitor genuinely wished to read Jacobus' account of St Giles' life; the visitor was writing a guide to the county's literary treasures, or an account of Jacobus' works in Britain, or a life of Jacobus; or he was sent by a firm of dealers to make comparisons with another example of the work; or he wished to take photographs for his private album; or he planned to steal it under the bishop's nose; or he distracted the bishop in his study while an accomplice raided the library; or he simply wished to handle an incunabulum for the first time in his life.'

'I take your point, sir – although I feel obliged to comment that not all of your suggestions are credible - but why bring the book down to the study and not leave it in the library?'

'Again, we could think of a number of reasons,' I replied confidently. 'The two would be more private in the study; or there was a fire in the study, whereas the library was unheated; or the lighting was better at the bishop's desk; or the study was more conducive to intimate conversation after the perusal of the volume than the library, which is no doubt large and shadowy; or the bishop was unwilling to be seen round the place in his visitor's company. None of that is really important at this stage, however. The bishop totters up to the library, gets the volume in question, tucks it carefully under his arm, re-descends the staircase and lays the volume carefully on the desk. The two men quarrel; the visitor takes the bishop by surprise; the bishop is pushed against the chimney-piece and dies; the killer dresses the scene up to look like an accident, waits until the castle is completely quiet and dark, and then makes his unseen exit. Although we cannot yet pinpoint motive, we have deduced the existence of a stranger on the premises on the night the bishop met his death: that's the important thing. We're probably going to get this wrapped up in next to no time!' Please, kindly reader, forgive the detective inspector his optimism.

Our next step was to clarify the castle routine. Our inquiries resulted in the following picture. Mostly non-resident members of the household were off the premises by six in the evening. Since the bishop rarely fixed appointments after that time, visitors were off the premises as well. The four resident members of the household - the bishop and his wife, the chaplain and the housekeeper - sat down to high tea at six; we also know that on this occasion the archdeacon had tea at the castle. Thereafter it was customary for them to disperse to activities of their choice: a meeting in the city, further work, some reading, a bit of television, perhaps, or, in the archdeacon's case, a short trip home. Both Mr Skyner and Mrs Wedlake occupied flats in the north wing, on different floors. Generally the bishop and his wife made a point of meeting again at nine, so that the last hour and a half or two hours of the day could be spent in their own company. Supper was always available in the kitchen for those who desired it. Occasionally the bishop would work late, that is, return to his study to fill the day's dying hours. In this case he would, when ready, retire to a spare bedroom set aside for this purpose, so as not to disturb his wife in the marital bedroom. The housekeeper locked the house when the secretary had indicated, on his daily sheet of events, that no further visitors were anticipated. Security was a consideration when valuable books and confidential documents were in question. As we knew already, the secretary, the almoner and the archdeacon had keys to a discreet door in the north wing, in case they had business after the castle was locked for the night.

All this explained why a visitor could be admitted late at night without attracting notice; and how Mrs Wyndham-Brookes would not necessarily notice her husband's prolonged absence at night. I had already deduced that, because the only study key available to us was the one found in the lock, the murderer had simply helped himself to one of the two habitually hanging inside the study-door. The keys to the study door that led from the salon were kept in the study itself, under the bishop's control, although, as we have learnt, he had never been known to use them, and they were not made accessible to the housekeeper, because there was no need for her to lock or unlock his lordship's study.

In all this, I keep referring to our mysterious visitor as a male, but we were fully aware that a woman could just as easily fit the bill. In history, male malefactors probably outweigh the female of the species, but I was not going to allow this to influence my assessment of the situation before us. Why should a woman be less likely to read Middle French and to have an interest in a thirteenth-century work of hagiography than a man? For all we knew, the Jacobus volume was a blind, the only Middle French required being to decipher SAINT GILLES ABBE at the start of the chapter devoted to that saint.

There were several other points we needed to clarify, so I asked the chaplain about celebration of the festal day in the bishop's household.

'Mr Skyner,' I began, 'at your initial interviews, you and others seemed fairly conversant with the details of St Giles' life and with the fact that it is celebrated on 1 September. Could you tell us how this is?'

'Well, as you know, inspector, his lordship regarded himself as, and was known to be, a catholic Anglican, differing from Rome only on one or two points of doctrine and practice. Even without that, I suppose, as Anglicans we should have at least nodded in the direction of St Giles on 1 September. There are two other things I should perhaps point out to you, inspector. The first is that his lordship was born with one leg shorter than the other, so that it was obvious to his parents that he would limp through life - literally. The other is that his parents named him after the patron saint of cripples, in the hope, I've no doubt, that the saint's protection would allow young Giles Wyndham-Brookes to lead a perfectly normal life. In the event, the shortness of the one leg was corrected by surgery in his childhood – a bit of judicious stretching with calipers, I understand – and in adulthood you would not have noticed a limp in his lordship. Now the bishop attributed this recovery to the intercession of his name-saint, and he maintained a fondness for the saint throughout his life. On the feast-day, therefore, he would celebrate the Mass of St Giles in the cathedral or in the castle chapel, whichever was deemed more appropriate at the time, and he would order a sort of banquet for the main meal of the day, at which a small number of people with walking infirmities were invited to join the household. An essential ingredient at the meal was the *soupe basque* associated with St Giles. Don't ask me for a recipe, but I know it contains dried beans, onion, pumpkin, cabbage and garlic! At this meal it was his lordship's custom to make a short speech – to mark the solemnity of the occasion – invariably including in it an outline of the saint's life. Anyone, therefore, who had been only a short while in the household would be familiar with the nature of the occasion. Does that answer your question?'

'It does, thank you.'

Feeling that the atmosphere at the castle was becoming a little overheated, I decided that we needed a larger picture. This would enable us to take a cooler, wider view – I fondly thought! With this in mind, Hewitt and I returned to Worcester that afternoon to have a few words with the diocesan chancellor. As I understood it, the chancellor fulfils much the same role in a diocese as the clerk does on a school's governing board. My reasoning was that, of all officials at The Old Palace, where the diocesan offices were, he would be the most likely to have his finger on the pulse.

The chancellor of Worcester diocese, Revd Mr Guy Wellingthorpe, was a sturdy man of fifty, greying at the temples, sallow of feature, intelligent of eye, with a pointed nose and a jutting chin. He doubled up (as we later learnt) as vicar of St Peter's in the city. News of the bishop's death had reached The Old Palace, as was only natural, and I imagined that arrangements were already being made for the funeral, that provisional systems of management were being put in place, and that the administration was making all necessary adjustments. I realised that in a sense we were in the way, but we needed more information, and there would never be, for us, a better time. When Mr Wellingthorpe, Hewitt and I had accordingly made ourselves comfortable in his office – a north-giving room cluttered with papers and stray books and overflowing ash-trays and heavy with the odour of stale tobacco – I asked him whether it was conceivable that Bishop Wyndham-Brookes had been the target of an evangelical fanatic.

'Ooh, dear,' he said, 'that's a very wide question! All things are possible in theory, I suppose, but I really couldn't say offhand whether that was even a remote possibility.'

'Just rehearse for us, if you would,' I said, 'the bishop's position in the Church of England.'

'Even that's a very big question, inspector, and one difficult to answer with any accuracy. You see, while it is possible to speak with Church leaders and sound their opinions, and while it is possible to gauge to some extent the opinions of those filling the pews each Sunday, blanket judgements are bound to be approximate at best, misleading at worst. Furthermore, I am really familiar only with this small corner of the Church.'

'That's probably all we need,' I countered. 'If you give us the local picture, we can then at least place our suspects in some sort of context.'

'So you already have suspects in mind, inspector?'

'No, not really: just everyone at Hartlebury Castle, for a start! but we're looking more widely than that.'

'All right, then, but only on the understanding that my remarks are not to be pressed too far. May I ask whether you are a church-goer, inspector?'

'Yes, C of E, by upbringing and by inclination.'

'Then much of what I say will already be familiar to you, I've no doubt. This is how I see it. The Church's origin at the time of Henry VIII was really a mistake, but that doesn't detract from the rightness of the Church's cause today. The trouble was, while it had broken with Rome, it did not embrace Reform: it was neither fish nor fowl, and that uncertainty has persisted into the twentieth century. Some have likened the Anglican Church to a pantomime horse, and the image has a certain truth: it looks like a single animal, and for much of the time it functions as a single animal, but the two halves are only loosely connected and have a constant tendency to go their own ways. Some are happy with this state of uneasy coexistence, some would prefer to replace it with something a little more stable – and more convincing! I shall come to that in a minute. Of course, others prefer the image of a whirligig or roundabout: plenty of movement but going precisely nowhere, just round and round! But to return to our horse: the left wing of the Church – if I may so phrase it, for the sake of the present discussion – leans towards Lutheranism, if not Calvinism. That is to say, in matters of doctrine, nothing is to be accepted which does not arise directly from the Scriptures. So, no purgatory, no Marian dogmas, no papal infallibility, no cult of the saints, no sacramentals, as the Romans call them, and so forth. In matters of worship, things are to be kept simple, straightforward, readily understandable – none of this Latin stuff! – with an emphasis on the Word of God and its exposition in a homily. In matters of morals, strict adherence to the Ten Commandments and the Sermon on the Mount is required. In matters of piety, the Christian will develop a personal relationship with God in confident prayer, without the trappings of beads, relics, novenas, pilgrimages, candles, processions, sacramentals and such like.

'The right wing of the Church – to continue our metaphor – leans towards Rome. We can repeat our division of Christian life so that a direct comparison is possible, So, in matters of doctrine, anything that can be reasoned to from Scripture, the Fathers and the first eight councils of the Church is to be accepted. Some mariology and some hagiography are acceptable. Other popish doctrines are probably tolerable if not insisted on as touchstones of orthodoxy. As regards public worship, moderate flamboyance, if I may so phrase it, visual aids and manifestations of proper devotion are acceptable. In morals, reason is allowed a role. There is a recognition, for example, that the Decalogue is not principally a Christian, but a Jewish, code, and that the *New* Testament is the well from which to draw instruction for Christian living. And finally, in matters of piety, many popish practices make sense and can be helpful.

'Now the tension between the extreme left and the extreme right can prove intolerable, to the point where a strict evangelical Anglican will refuse to speak to a Romanising catholic Anglican: I kid you not. For some, the tension is such that they fall off the end of the spectrum, moving over either to Protestantism – into one of the non-conformist Churches, for example – or to Roman Catholicism. What about those who choose to remain in the Church?

'Well, here a bit of theology is necessary. What the Church suffers from – I use the word advisedly – is coexistence. The spectrum of belief and practice is so broad that anything definite or anything deemed *essential* and therefore to be insisted on threatens to upset the delicate equilibrium. The result, say some, is a mishmash of ill-thought-out doctrines that are vague because they need to satisfy everyone; and because they are vague, they cannot be true – or false either, I suppose. Thus the Anglican Church could give the impression that not only does it not know what it believes, but that it doesn't really *matter* what it believes, provided that people are willing to rub along together. As regards practice, the Book of Common Prayer provides a basis, but *Common Worship* now provides alternatives in modern English, so, from one point of view, unity is not really achieved, except in so far as all worship has to be approved by the Church Assembly. The same church often provides different kinds of worship to satisfy the wishes of different groups, and so you have different congregations, using the same building, whose connection is only tenuous. In morals, agreement on such matters as divorce, euthanasia and gambling is lacking, but generally tolerance prevails. Here I should mention the so-called liberal wing of the Anglican Church, except that, since it's in the middle, it can hardly be a wing! Liberal Anglicans, sometimes called the broad Church, wish to see a loosening up of doctrine, ethics and worship, and there is a certain justice on their side. What we are coming to realise more and more forcefully, in the light of modern biblical scholarship, is that it is a grave mistake to refer to "New Testament theology", as if there were only one, and that the New Testament writers – the evangelists, Paul, James and so on – were agreed on it. No, it has become crystal clear that there are as many differences within the New Testament as there are writers. May I give you just two examples?

'Matthew insists that remarriage after divorce is impossible: the couple are united in matrimony for life, whereas, in 1 Corinthians, Paul allows it. Matthew and Mark seem to believe in a Real Presence in the eucharist, however they would have defined it, whereas Luke and Paul seem to believe more in a symbolic or spiritual presence of the Lord. I could go on, but the argument is that if the New Testament itself is divided on matters of belief - and practice, I should add – it is not incumbent on the Anglican Church to achieve, much less impose, a false unity. Christians must be allowed to respond to the person of Jesus in any way that they find comfortable, within certain limits, of course.

'However, some members of the Church who are open-minded but not liberal prefer to explore another approach. Their argument is that, instead of remaining satisfied with coexistence, with all its shortcomings, the Church should be aiming at a *synthesis*, a genuine, dialectical merger of thesis and antithesis which would be more powerful than either separately. Here, in Anglicanism, a combination of evangelicalism (or Protestantism) and catholicism (or popery) would be won and would act as a model for the future unity of Christians world-wide. However, I think I have allowed myself to stray from the topic in hand!

'So, the Bishop of Worcester. Four events this year have combined to rock the Church of England, and his lordship went public on all of them, thus exposing himself to the slings and arrows of all who disagree with him. I take them in no particular order.

'Firstly, women priests. The trouble really began in 1944, when Bishop Hall of Hong Kong ordained a woman priest. Both Canterbury and York repudiated the act, and later, in 1948, the Lambeth Conference forbade Hong Kong to go ahead with any more such ordinations. The debate, and the resentment, however, rumbled on. Then earlier this year, the House of Bishops received a report they commissioned last year – 1965 - called *The Proper Place of Women in the Church* – I think I've got that right - and Bishop Wyndham-Brookes went on record as opposing not just the possibility but the very discussion of the possibility of ordaining women to the priesthood. This boldness won him some enemies from the liberal and evangelical schools in the Church.

'Connected with that is the second event: the Bishop Pike affair. Let me explain if you are not familiar with this. James Pike, fifth bishop of California and now in his early fifties, has been known for some time as a radical and open thinker – an iconoclast, some would call him – who challenges many accepted beliefs in the Church: he has said publicly that what the Church needs is more belief and fewer beliefs. Nice one, James! He appears on television in the States, and gives many interviews, and is generally very well known in America. Now earlier this year he ordained a deaconess as deacon. In other words, he placed an ecclesiastical assistant into the ranks of the clergy. It is his outspoken views on doctrinal matters, however, which have set him particularly at loggerheads with his fellow-bishops. Several times he has appealed for a heresy trial, so that his views can be aired and tested. Finally, earlier this year, although there was not a formal heresy trial, a committee of eleven met to consider his views. The committee stopped short of advocating his expulsion from the Church, but it did brand his more controversial views as "offensive" and "irresponsible".

Of course, his personal life-style hasn't helped his case with people like our own late bishop. Bishop Wyndham-Brookes publicly suggested a proper heresy trial, excommunication and possibly defrocking as well!

'The third event is the meeting of the Archbishop of Canterbury with Pope Paul VI on 23 March this year. It is so recent that I need say very little about it, but just let me fill you in on the late bishop's part. The Archbishop of Canterbury invited him to chair the preliminary meeting of Anglicans that was to lead to a preliminary meeting of the Anglicans with the Romans, and the committee's remit was to identify the main areas of difference and so the main areas of discussion. My understanding is that the bishop was loath to accept but was persuaded to by members of his household. There was some jocular reference to St Giles as a model ecumenist: did he not embrace monasticism, as the Romans do, and yet perform miracles as evangelicals would like to do?! The bishop's acceptance meant a series of meetings, in London and here in Worcester, with other members of the committee, but in the event only one of these had taken place before the bishop's untimely death.

'And finally you may remember the Lloyd-Jones' trumpet call a month or two back.'

'That rings a bell,' I said. 'Just refresh my memory, will you?'

'Certainly, inspector. Dr Martyn Lloyd-Jones is a Welsh preacher on the evangelical wing, now in his mid- or late sixties, I suppose, and well-known for the last twenty years as pastor of Westminster Chapel in London. His fiery sermons, which do not often last less than an hour, attract hundreds of listeners, many of them young. They always expound a text of scripture. On the occasion to which I refer, he was not in his own church but addressing a meeting of the National Assembly of Evangelicals. He issued a stern invitation to evangelical clergy who belong to Churches in which evangelicals and liberals co-exist to leave their Church in favour of a denomination that is more biblically based. The Christian press rang with the controversy that ensued, but a widespread reaction from fellow-Anglicans was that his stance was extreme and should not be supported. In a letter to the *Church Times*, Bishop Wyndham-Brookes made the point that the very genius of the Anglican Church is that it can hold together evangelicals, liberals and catholics in a working and fruitful union; to cluster together in like-minded groups is to form sects that don't speak to each other: is, in a word, to be unbiblical. Although his remarks were to be expected, many evangelicals felt that he should have given more support to their point of view, for example, by commending them for their emphasis on the role of the Spirit in the Christian life, for their reverence for scripture, or for their simplicity in worship.'

'So how has all this become a threat to the bishop, if that is what you are driving at?'

'This is my reading of the situation, inspector. The bishop is not a danger to non-conformists: he is not a member of their Church, and he is engaged in debates that are on the very fringe of their consciousness. On the other hand he *is* a danger to Anglicans who have come to regard him as a threat to the unity of their Church. If he should succeed in bringing about union with Rome – he and others, of course - where does that leave the evangelicals? Presumably tagging along somewhere in the rear, unregarded, second-class or even third-class citizens. The catchword is "united but not absorbed", but that doesn't satisfy evangelicals, who will be on the tail-end of any unification process.'

The picture was now much clearer to us – I think! but I was left in no doubt that the Anglican Church, inherently unstable, was heading for a schism somewhere along the line. Perhaps, however, I should not be meddling beyond my competence!

SIX

Before we left, and enjoining the utmost discretion, I asked the chancellor for suggestions of parishes which harboured fervent evangelical ministers. His answer required considerable thought. There were, he told us, 280-odd churches in the diocese, with about the same number of clergy. He could not claim to be familiar with them all, but he eventually selected eight whom he regarded as, in his words, 'rabidly evangelical'. After some rapid telephone calls, of these eight Hewitt and I eliminated six, on grounds of ill-health, age or absence. This left two – I hesitate to use the word – 'suspects', whom we proceeded to visit that very evening, dividing our forces for maximum efficiency. It fell to Hewitt to interview the Revd Thomas Wilkes, incumbent of St Nicholas, Warndon, on the north-western outskirts of the city, while I was to visit the Revd Gus Crabtree at All Saints, on Deansway in the city. The results of my own interview follow shortly. There was a surprise in store for both of us.

Here follows Hewitt's report (in which I have taken it upon myself to correct one or two grammatical and orthographical errors: edikation ain't what it was in *my* youth).

Inspector Wickfield instructed me to visit the Revd Wilkes at Warndon, and I was of course happy to do so. In a spirit of meek obedience' [not to say obsequiousness!], 'I have endeavoured to reproduce the inspector's orotund and meticulous style as being admirably suited to the matter in hand. I was sad to see that a lot of the area I drove through is disappearing under housing: I understand that, in all, four working farms are earmarked for destruction.

However, the church remains, and it is both pretty and interesting, with a very unusual timber-framed bell-tower. The incumbent was expecting my visit: a large, rubicund man, with a cheerful face and an extravert manner, hair greying at the edges, casually – *very* casually – dressed. He put me at my ease at once with a pressing invitation to partake of a cup of tea, which I gladly accepted in the manner of my leader. I asked him first, when we were seated in his study, to tell me something about himself.

'Me, sergeant? Very little to tell. After school, I went to Oak Hill College, in north central London, to do a three year BA (Hons) degree in theological and pastoral studies. My first post was as curate at Christ Church, Clifton – that was quite a challenge, but I enjoyed my ten years there. Then I moved to St George's in Tiverton, a bit further down the West Country, and I was curate there for five years – that was good too - before moving to Christ Church, Blackburn, as vicar. You can imagine that the change from a small town in Devon to a large conurbation in Lancashire was something of a shock to the system, but I have to say the parishioners were very welcoming and enthusiastic. After fifteen years there, I moved here eight years ago, and I hope not to have to move again! What else can I tell you?'

'What is evangelicalism? I'm sorry to sound so dim, Mr Wilkes, but the inspector and I seem to be drowning in a sea of labels.'

'Then the answer to your question is going to make matters even worse! You see, terms are flung about here, there and everywhere, and people attach different meanings to them at different times. Let me give you an example. I have recently read three different attempts to categorise the spectrum which evangelicals inhabit: one categorisation is charismatic, mainstream and broad evangelicals; according to another, there are traditionalist, centrist and modernist evangelicals; and a third division is into conservative, open and illuminative or born-again evangelicals. If you understand evangelicalism as a position midway between liberalism and fundamentalism, you also have liberal and fundamentalist evangelicals at either end; and I haven't mentioned the neo-evangelicals. All in all, it's a bit of a cauldron.'

'OK,' I said, 'following all that up is obviously counterproductive for our present purposes. It looks as if the evangelical wing of the Anglican Church is in complete disarray! Is there anything people agree on?'

'Oh, yes,' he said, 'but as you imply, it is only essentials – and even there ...

'Well, evangelicalism is usually summed up in the so-called Three Solas: *sola scriptura, sola gratia* and *sola fide.* All this fancy Latin means is that evangelicals accept the Bible as the sole authoritative source of truth; God's grace as the only source of the Christian life; and trust in God as the only worthy response.'

'What I don't see,' I pursued, ever mindful of my mentor's inquiring and restless mind, 'is why evangelicals stay in the Anglican Church at all: why not go the whole hog and become Protestants?'

'That's because they value liturgy and historical continuity, but principally, I suppose – and here I can speak out of personal conviction – they don't wish to lapse into mere sectarianism, if I may use the word without denigrating my Protestant brothers and sisters.'

'And how did you regard Bishop Wyndham-Brookes, with his highchurch ways?'

'Somewhat ambivalently, if the truth be told, sergeant. When I saw him last night – '

'What: you saw him last night?' I cried out in astonishment.

'Yes, I had an appointment with him after supper. Why do you ask?'

'You had an appointment with the bishop, at Hartlebury? Why on earth didn't you say so beforehand?'

'You never asked me, sergeant. How was I to know that I was expected to come out with this?'

'Right, please tell me from the beginning. You may have very important evidence.'

'Evidence? No, I can't help you with his death at all: sorry. Well, the bishop phoned me up a few days ago and asked for a meeting. He said that he was exercised in his mind over the way the Church of England was going, and he wanted to consult different members of the clergy to canvas their views on the basis of their different backgrounds and beliefs. I was flattered to think that he obviously regarded me as in some way a spokesman for the evangelical cause. He said that the meeting was informal, there was no particular agenda, nobody taking minutes, but he would value my opinions. So along I went. We met in his study, over several hours, and we discussed four main items, but you won't want to know about them, sergeant: just too dull for a busy policeman!'

'At what time did you leave?'

'I'm not sure: about ten, probably.'

'And how was he when you left?'

'How was he? How should he be? Perfectly all right, as far as I could tell, although clearly a troubled man. You asked me what my attitude to him was. As I was saying, when I met him last night, he was the soul of affability, and I took that at face value, but I had an unworthy suspicion, quite unfounded, I'm sure, that his real purpose in calling for the meeting was to soften up the evangelical wing before proceeding full tilt – well, as fast as circumstances would allow – to union with Rome. It would not be in his or the Church's interest to see the third of Anglicans who are evangelical disappear away to the left in disgust, but I'm not sure how genuine his interest in evangelical concerns was. He said at one point in the evening that he regarded evangelicalism as anti-intellectual because it puts such emphasis on sentiment, inner feeling. It was only a passing comment, but I got the impression that he rather looked down on us evangelicals as lacking in intellectual rigour.'

'In that case why is his secretary, as I understand the matter, an evangelical?'

'Ah, that, I've heard it said, is a sop to left-wing opinion. The secretary has no influence on policy or theology: he just tinkers about with the paperwork – diary, mail, meeting agendas, that sort of thing – so an evangelical in that position can do no harm!'

'Did you regard the bishop as a danger to the Church?'

'You mean, did I murder him? No, I didn't, since you ask, sergeant, but that doesn't mean I didn't regard his manoeuvres towards Rome as a grave mistake. He risked damaging the consistency and coherence of 400 years of Anglicanism.'

'Tell me, did you notice a copy of a leather-bound incunabulum on his desk?'

'No, we sat facing the fire, and I had my back to the desk.'

'Did you notice anything unusual about the room, or his demeanour?'

'No. Of course, if I'd known he was going to be murdered, I might have taken more notice!'

I couldn't get anything further out of Mr Wilkes – nothing of interest, I mean – so I came away with the conviction that he could not help us very much. End of Sgt Hewitt's report.'

I follow this with an account of my own interview with the Revd Crabtree. His church, All Saints on Deansway, has an interesting history, possibly going back to Saxon times, but the present building is Georgian – and handsome and central. My impression, from opening skirmishes (so to speak) in our acquaintance, was that the ministerial team is trying very hard to reach the people of Worcester; whether they wish to be reached is another matter. I arrived as the minister and his wife and two children were finishing their evening meal, but they were very hospitable and welcoming. Gus Crabtree ushered me into his study so that we could converse privately. Large notices, such as 'Let go, let God', 'Upward, inward, outward' and 'Spirit-led, not tradition-bound', adorned his walls and proclaimed his religious affiliations. His age? Mid- to late thirties, I should have said; a crisp, clean, handsome face; jovial but earnest simultaneously; warm and enthusiastic. I took to the man. However, I was there not to pass the time of day but on business: was there any feeling in the – I nearly said 'lower end' but changed that to 'more evangelical arm' – of the diocese that the bishop was a danger to the Church's continued well-being?

'Well, inspector,' he began in reply, 'there is no concealing that Anglicanism is going through a difficult time – except that people have probably been saying that since the 1530s! Tensions are erupting all over the place, and feelings run high. Where religion is concerned, people can all too easily believe themselves commissioned by the Almighty to purge the Church, or bear dramatic witness – perhaps like St Simeon the Stylite and his fellows – or go to extremes. Some believe that a split is inevitable – over women priests, for example – while others strain every nerve to keep the organism functioning as a unit. There are undoubtedly some who saw in Bishop Wyndham-Brookes' fostering of relations with Rome a sell-out of Anglicanism: a sort of monstrous betrayal that threatened all that Anglicanism stood for.'

'And you ?' I asked.

'Well, he at least had the grace to canvass my opinion, so he seemed aware of dangers to the unity of Anglicanism.'

'Forgive my saying so, Mr Crabtree, but you are very young to be canvassed by the bishop!'

'Yes, you might think so, inspector, but I was only one of four invited over for consultation.'

'What, recently?

'Yes, last night, as a matter of fact.'

'Last night?' I asked in some bewilderment. 'You saw the bishop last night?'

'Yes, why is that so surprising, inspector? Four of us outspoken evangelical clergy were invited for an "informal consultation" – the bishop's own words – but in the event only two of us were able to make it: Tom Wilkes from Warndon and myself.'

'And what did you talk about, if I may ask?'

'The bishop was kind enough to share his worries with us. He said he was not looking for advice, but he wanted opinions other than his own, particularly from people in the Church whose views he could not fully share. He realised that the move to ordain women as priests threatened union with Rome: but was it right in itself? While he sympathised with some of what Bishop James Pike of California stood for, he couldn't accept Pike's actions: did we? He wanted to further union with Rome, but he wondered whether the bishops would ever succeed in carrying evangelicals with them. And finally he was worried by Lloyd-Jones' call to evangelical clergy to leave the Church and move over to non-conformism: would we obey the call?'

'I see; and what were your replies?'

'May I just go back a bit in time, inspector? You may have heard of Charles Simeon, a vigorous preacher who died in the 1830s in his late seventies: a remarkable man, in my opinion. His published sermon notes run to over twenty volumes, but that is by the bye. Now Simeon, an out-and-out, rank evangelical, who was vicar of Holy Trinity Church in Cambridge for over fifty years, was asked how he could stay in a Church which had not treated him well but dismissed him as an enthusiast and fanatic who elevated Scripture above organisation and tradition. He is said to have answered that he valued Holy Communion, because it was his first Holy Communion as an undergraduate at Cambridge that had brought him enlightenment, and that he valued membership of the Church: he had no wish to hide himself in a sect, and it was only as an Anglican that he could effectively promote missionary work abroad. Now when I was an undergraduate at Cambridge, I stumbled across a copy of Simeon's *Memoirs*, edited by a man called Carus – a pretty hefty volume, I may say – and I took to reading large extracts from it from time to time. Of course, it is very dated now, but it is not surprising that it still enthuses someone who aspires to be a preacher. One thing in particular struck me. The preface to his second volume of sermons is given in full, and it includes the three criteria which Simeon intends should inform his preaching: does it humble the sinner, exalt the Saviour and promote holiness? "If in any one single instance it loses sight of any of these points, let it be condemned without mercy," he comments. I was so impressed by this sentiment that I determined to take it as the informing principle of my own preaching. Now if the principles on which one bases one's preaching – and ministry - are as broad as this, it is not always possible to come to ready conclusions about the many problems the modern world throws at us: one needs time for reflection, prayer, discussion with others. My opinions on the questions his lordship raised last night are therefore provisional and in some case possibly ill-formed. Sorry: am I being a bit wordy? Let me get on.

'Evangelicals have no one view on the ordination of women, although probably most oppose it – as I do, on the grounds that its foundation in scripture is doubtful. The Bishop Pike affair is similar: Billy Graham has supported him, but most evangelicals, including myself, feel uncomfortable with him. His views would gain more adherence if they were expressed in more measured tones and as the fruit of a more measured life-style. As regards union with Rome, virtually all evangelicals oppose it – unless, of course, Rome gives up its many errors. I can't see myself ever welcoming union with Rome unless it is a very relaxed and undemanding relationship, which is unlikely. And Dr Lloyd-Jones has not, so far, managed to sway evangelical clergy like myself, probably for the reasons given above when I mentioned Charles Simeon. Does that help?'

'Admirably. Now can I ask whether you noticed anything unusual about last night?'

'Unusual? How "unusual"?'

'Did the bishop seem himself?'

'Yes. That is to say, to all appearances all was normal, but over the evening – and we were there for nearly two hours, I should say – I got the impression that the bishop was finding life a bit tiring. I should not have been surprised to learn that he was weighing up whether to fight on for the improvement of the Anglican Church or to retire early. He was just testing how severe a fight he would have on his hands if he were radically out of step with his evangelical clergy.'

'Do you know who the other two clergy invited were?'

'Yes, and I know that certainly one of them pretended to have a previous appointment so that he wouldn't have to meet the bishop.'

'Oh?'

'He had heard that the bishop dismissed Anglican evangelicals, and evangelicals in general, I suppose, as quarrelsome, bigoted and narrow-minded, given to intolerance and puritanism. That is not a sentiment designed to endear a third of his Church! So the vicar stayed away.'

'Out of interest, how would you answer the bishop's charge?'

'A difficult question, that, inspector. May I ask where your own sympathies lie?'

'In religious matters, I presume you mean.'

'Yes.'

'I am content to be broad Church, perhaps hovering on the borders of liberalism and Anglo-Catholicism, if such labels mean anything.'

'Then you may not be familiar with the extreme wing of evangelicalism. I think that perhaps some evangelicals do err on the side of intolerance. Calvinism contains more than a streak of bigotry and dour austerity. Mainstream evangelicals, however, are not made of such tart stuff. Let me tell you this, inspector, although it may smack of self-satisfaction! A recent psychological profile of evangelical clergy came to the conclusion that on the whole male evangelical clergy are, and I quote, "tender-minded and stable extraverts" – not bad, eh? Evangelicals claim merely to focus on Christian essentials – the Word of God, worship, mission, personal holiness – and to leave aside historical accretions that cannot be squared with the Bible. That's hardly the stuff of extremism and prejudice, is it?'

'So can you see any member of an extreme evangelical cell plotting to do away with the bishop?'

'Well, I suppose an extreme evangelical is more likely than an extreme Anglo-Catholic, but you seem to be presuming, if I may say so, that the killer is a religious fanatic: couldn't it have been a personal enemy?'

'It could, of course, but we are pursuing the religious thread in the first instance because of a book lying on the bishop's desk.'

'A book?'

'Yes, the bishop's chaplain seemed to think it was odd to find a book in Middle French on the bishop's desk when he can't read Middle French. Its presence therefore suggests a visitor with an interest in, or knowledge of, medieval hagiography; but we're keeping an open mind.'

'What book was it, may I ask?'

'Jacobus de Voragine's *Legenda Aurea,* with which you are no doubt better acquainted than I am.'

'I can assure you, inspector, that no such book was on the bishop's desk while we were there. I know that because I used the desk at one point to draw up a short memorandum, and there was nothing on it but little piles of papers. There's one other thing about fanatical evangelicals, inspector, to revert to our previous subject. An evangelical who remains a member of the Anglican Church has already demonstrated moderation and restraint: if he were, as one might say, extreme, he would long ago have departed to a non-conformist Church of his choice. In my view, therefore, you are pursuing a false trail. In any case, the more extreme the evangelical, the less truck he is going to have with medieval hagiography, with all its excesses, fantasy and credulousness!'

'You're probably right, Mr Crabtree. Thank you for your time, and I wish your ministry every success!'

It remained for Hewitt and me to compare notes when we reconvened at the station late that evening over a last cup of tea. We were both tired but satisfied that the day had been fruitful. We had investigated the scene of the crime, outlined some questions and come to certain conclusions, interviewed the six principal members of the castle household, consulted the chancellor of the diocese and spoken with two members of the diocesan clergy who had been with the bishop on the evening of his death. What was Hewitt's reaction so far?

'Well, sir, I should say that we are faced with more questions than answers. It is difficult at this stage to identify what might be important. For example, is the medieval book – the incunab something – relevant? is the feast-day of St Giles relevant? can we be absolutely certain it was murder? if it was, are we satisfied that the members of the household are in the clear? or, on the contrary, is one of them more likely than the others to be the culprit? what are we to make of our amiable evangelical friends?'

'Yes,' I agreed, 'all a bit baffling at the moment. However, I think we can be certain it was murder – and the pathologist's report may be of interest in that regard – and I have also come to realise, if I had not realised before, that a man in Bishop Wyndham-Brookes' position is vulnerable to all sorts of oddballs. We are dealing with someone cunning and determined, but I'm not sure whether the study set-up is sending us, and the world, a message – and if so, what? – or is neutral. We have already been offered three different applications of the St Giles' legend to the bishop's death: his lordship was shown particular contempt by being killed when he was on the edge of great advancement; he was eliminated as a punishment for egregious lack of ambition; he was moving over to Rome and taking the Anglican Church with him and had to be stopped. That's quite a spread of meaning already!'

The pathologist's report, of which I give you a summary here, reached us the following morning. There was much technical detail, but the gist of it was that the bishop had been struck very forcefully across the front of the head, once, with a metal object, like a poker, and then laid immediately in the hearth. According to the pathologist, simply falling on to the fender would not have produced so great a wound, although he could not exclude the possibility altogether. Death occurred at approximately midnight. Our own team had picked up on several further points: if the poker had been used, it had been wiped clean; and it looked as if blood from the bishop's head had been, or at least could have been, smeared artificially on to the fender.

SEVEN

In my uncertainty, I began to cast about for other reasons why the bishop should have been murdered. Was it a case of theft? I imagined a different scene from the one I had been working on. Assuming that the Jacobus was immaterial, I conjured up a vision of the bishop in his study on the night in question. His two clerical visitors had departed, he is preparing to retire to bed, he is confronted by an intruder. The man, a chance prowler who has seen two men leave the premises and has taken advantage of a door left unlocked behind them, demands money from the bishop and pushes the bishop, who falls. Then, however, why does not he not just flee? how could he have set up the locked room mystery without preamble? No, that reconstruction would not do. Try again. An unhinged antiquarian has been plotting for a long time to steal the bishop's famed St Porchaire tazza (if he has one); he inhabits a book-strewn house in deepest Worcester, with three cats and a tame monkey. Having previously visited the bishop on some specious pretext and stolen one of the study keys, he returns to the castle, prepared to break in. Two men exit, as he waits in the bushes, and he seizes his chance. When he unexpectedly intrudes on the bishop preparing his next sermon in the study and is challenged, he strikes out and is horrified to see the prelate fall to his death on the rug. He swiftly puts his escape plan into operation and leaves the castle, abandoning his precious booty. No, all too fanciful: he's made of sterner stuff than to panic just because he has launched a bishop on his final journey. In any case, why prepare to leave a locked-room mystery behind, when all he had to do was walk off with the tazza? He could not have anticipated killing the bishop in the course of his burglary. Try once more. The bishop's brother is thirsting to revenge a childhood slight. He makes an appointment for late in the evening, since he is anxious not to be seen on the premises; his excuse is to toast the bishop on his saint's-day. At a suitable moment, having got his grievance off his chest, he lashes out at his brother with a swipe of the poker, calmly puts the locked-room routine into operation and escapes undetected, leaving the police baffled behind him. Well, yes, certainly baffled.

Hewitt and I returned to Hartlebury Castle, ostensibly to go over all the events again, checking our facts and our logic (the little of it that there was), but in reality for want of any other ideas. This was early on the following morning. Knowing that the secretary reported for work at eight, and guessing that he would be at his post even on a Saturday, in view of the previous day's events, to let us in, we drove through the gates a little after eight on a cloudy and drizzly morning, more reminiscent of mid-autumn than of late summer. The castle looked sombre. The leaves of the virginia creeper were already turning, and they dripped with moisture. In response to our ring, the chaplain appeared at the door.

'Good heavens, inspector, that was quick,' he said.

'Quick?' I countered. 'What do you mean?'

'I've only just phoned the station to tell you of the latest tragedy. I've hardly put the phone down!'

'Please explain: we're completely in the dark.'

'Didn't you get my message? The secretary has hanged himself.'

'What?' I expostulated in my astonishment. 'You mean Mr Stringer?'

'Yes, yes, Simon Stringer: who else could I mean?'

'Please tell us about it.'

By this time we were all in the hall, and an agitated Mrs Wedlake had appeared from the castle's nether regions to join us.

'I had gone back to my room after breakfast,' the chaplain said, 'and I noticed from the window that the secretary's car was parked in the yard by the north wing. I was a little surprised, as it's Saturday, but I was pleased to have another member of staff on the premises to deal with correspondence and other matters and to help with the funeral arrangements. We should in due course, I've no doubt, have gone on to The Old Palace for further consultations. However, when I reached the study, Stringer was nowhere in sight, which I thought strange, as he had no other base in the castle. So I went out to the car park to see whether all was well, and lo and behold, there he was, poor man, hanging from a tree by the moat. I rushed to get a knife, cut him down and searched for signs of life: nothing. Gone. I immediately phoned for a doctor and to you. That's about all I can tell you, inspector: I haven't had time to do anything else.'

This latest development was so unexpected that I was momentarily paralysed. Taking a firm grip of myself, however, in the best Wickfield tradition, I asked to see the body. Skyner and Mrs Wedlake had carried it through the hallway in the north wing to a parlour on the ground floor. Simon Stringer looked as melancholy in death as he had in life, and I was stricken with pity for a humourless and earnest man who had chosen to end a life he had come to regard as futile. How would his family take the news? I hoped for a letter of explanation, and I was not disappointed. In a long letter of farewell, stuffed into a white envelope in his pocket and addressed to his wife, the deceased clergyman had set out his despair, and I reproduce it for you here.

My darling Jean (it began)

I cannot go on. I have failed you and the children; I have failed the bishop; I have failed my God. May God have mercy on me in his unfailing pity. I take full responsibility for my actions, and I am going to give you an account of all I have suffered and been guilty of so that no one else is blamed. This letter will reach the police first, so that you will be supported when you read it.

You know that my childhood was unhappy. We lived on a remote Norfolk farm, with little human company apart from ourselves, and I found school a trial. The other children were energetic, sociable, outgoing, or so it seemed to me, while I was more than happy to read a book or dream away my time in solitude. I do not blame my parents for this: it was just the way I was made. At secondary school I was dismissed by the other pupils as a swot and ridiculed for my lack of interest in games. That's life, I suppose. I can't blame the children. I inhabited a world of fantasy peopled by extraordinary heroes and by unimaginable villains, all of whom were invariably defeated in the end: a world of make-believe in which good triumphed and the innocent won through, in which even little people were given credit for courage and goodness. My sister was quite different and seems to have enjoyed her childhood in the ' real' world.

When I went on to theological college, things improved, because studiousness was valued and lack of interest in games regarded as irrelevant. I read widely, and I came to believe that the Bible contained all the answers to the world' s problems if only we would study it carefully and read it properly. Here in this unique collection of religious writings was a new world: one of horrors and blood-lust and night-time terrors, of mutilations and stonings and massacres, but one straddled by a sovereign deity whose will was law and who brought truth and justice — in the end. I studied its contents enthusiastically: imaginative and fantastic stories, folk-lore, poetry of enormous beauty, hymns of praise and repentance, descriptions of tragic battles, pieces of homely advice — but above all, the deeds of an absolute God who would brook no rivals.

I had been brought up as an Anglican, with a purposeful structure and a formal liturgy and a coherent if ambiguous history, and nothing I read and no one I met could persuade me to abandon the Church of my youth in favour of some non-conformist sect. So I came to regard myself as a faithful, committed and comfortable evangelical Anglican, but I have to say that my inner life was plagued by doubt about my worthiness in putting myself forward for holy orders — except that I had no idea what else to do in life, and in any case I didn' t wish to do anything else.

My first appointment as a clergyman, as you know, was to St Lawrence' s church at Skellingthorpe, near Lincoln. The rector, Mr Tidsdale, and I got on fine, but I became increasingly awkward in my parish duties: I loathed meeting people, I hated preaching because I was so bad at it, and I knew that Mr Tidsdale was becoming increasingly frustrated with me. In Bible-study groups I used to ramble on because I had lots to say but couldn' t gauge the feelings of the group or pitch what I had to say at the right level. I preferred quiet study and lonely walks to being a pastor of souls. My letters home were peppered with expressions of self-dissatisfaction — even self-hate - as I tried to come to terms with my situation. So I would write things like, I only wish I could overcome this shyness in the pulpit, or, Why on earth can' t I be a man and run the parish groups properly, or, I' m no good as a curate, I' m a failure. I despised myself for not trusting in God; I prayed, and I prayed harder, but I sank into a pit of timidity and wallowed in self-loathing.

My state of mind must have worried my parents, because my sister Diana came to spend a few days at the vicarage, as our guest, to offer me support and, I suppose, consolation. Would that she had stayed a million miles away! What happened next is inexcusable: I have no one to blame but myself; I have suffered such pangs of conscience since, that life has been excruciating almost to the point of being intolerable. My God, my God, why could I not trust you more?

Diana was two years younger than me: petite, pretty, with a rich shock of black hair and an eye-catching figure. The boys at school used to flock round her; she was companionable and funny and chatty: everything I was not. She was always the centre of attention. On her first evening with us at Skellingthorpe, she wore a dress that revealed the top of smooth, white breasts, and for the first time in my life — I blush still to confess it - I looked on her not as my sister whom I' d always known but as a sexual partner. You see, I was innocent then: a virgin from my birth, but my reactions to the female body were those of any other man. Well, I will skate over the details of the events of that night. I was so low in my spirits that I blindly and insanely clutched at a moment of wild and unbridled passion. Diana felt sorry for me in my distress and went along with it. I tip-toed along to her bedroom, and our embrace was a celestial and ecstatic experience — to be followed, oh, so quickly, by a slough of self-loathing deeper and more intense than even I had experienced before. I cannot express my feelings. Suffice it to say that I nearly did away with myself in an agony of self-reproach. Diana knew my state of mind and talked me round, but the sound of our conversation in the middle of the night must have alerted the vicar to what had happened.

Diana left first thing in the morning — what she said to our parents by way of explanation I've no idea — and the vicar, in his kindness, told me that I could no longer continue as his curate but that he would help me to look for a situation away from Norfolk and better suited to my temperament. You see, I presumed he acknowledged some value in me as a clergyman, even though I could no longer see it myself. I became secretary to the Bishop of Carlisle, and it was there that I met you, my love: a retiring and self-effacing young woman who recognised a fellow-sufferer and took pity on me. You did me the inestimable favour of agreeing to be my wife. How I now regret joining you in marriage with a monster!

Should I have told you of my sin? The idea revolted me. The shame, the embarrassment, the dishonour of it: I couldn't. Perhaps I was weak. I feared for your reaction: no doubt, as for any right-thinking person, disgust and revulsion. I couldn't risk losing you, so I kept quiet. If I had confided in you, your gentleness and patience might have won me back to God. As it was. I nursed a viper of abhorrence in my own bosom and turned from the God of my youth. I can hardly bear to tell you these things, but I am determined to explain to you why I am saying farewell — my darling.

When the Bishop of Carlisle died, in 1962, I applied for my present post, as you know, and got it. Referees obviously valued some or most of what I had achieved, and I am grateful to Bishop Wyndham-Brookes for being kind enough to take me on. I believe I have served him faithfully and to the best of my poor ability. However, it came to my notice that he was aware of what I had done. This is what happened. He attended some meeting in London, and amongst others present was my first rector, Gordon Tidsdale. What exactly was said of course I don' t know, but Bishop Wyndham-Brookes spoke to me recently about the possibility of my looking for another post. I was shocked. " Am I not giving satisfaction, my lord?" I asked. " I am very happy here: I shouldn' t wish to leave your lordship' s employment." He was embarrassed, but eventually I wormed the reason out of him. It had come to his attention, he said, that an incestuous relationship had led to the termination of a previous post, and he was pre-empting a repetition. He felt uncomfortable working with a man with such a blemish on his record, and if the matter should ever come out, he would be at a loss to explain the matter to his accusers and to justify his continuing employment of me. He gave me three months to look for something else.

I have concealed this from you, my darling, because I could not burden you with further problems. I turned the matter over and over in my mind. I spent sleepless nights. I prayed. Gradually the makings of an idea dawned in my mind. I considered it from every angle, and eventually I decided that his

70

lordship' s death was the only thing that would give me peace. I therefore carried out experiments so that I could make his death appear to be an accident, and two nights ago I put my idea into operation. I knew of appointments the bishop had made informally with some evangelical clergymen, and telling you that I had a piece of work I just had to complete before the morning, I returned to the castle just as his visitors were going. The rest is known to the police.

I struggled through yesterday' s interview with Inspector Wickfield, but I cannot continue with the burden of this further crime on my conscience. I have not had a second' s peace since the bishop was felled in his own study, and I have determined to die by my own hand. Please forgive me. My fondest love to you and the children.

Your ever-loving and ever-sorrowful

Simon

When I had absorbed this poignant letter, I passed it over to Hewitt while I pondered its content. Hewitt turned to me.

'That's very sad,' he said. 'He struck me as a good man. Such a pity it has ended this way.'

'It's all wrong,' I replied.

'All wrong? What's wrong? He's told us why and how: he's confessed! What more could we want?'

'No, it's wrong,' I repeated. 'For a start, he originally told us, perhaps in an unguarded moment, that the bishop never locked his study door; now he tells us that he, Stringer, set up the supposedly realistic scene of an accident with the door deliberately locked! But more than that, his story doesn't ring true. I do not believe that the vicar of Skellingthorpe would have told anyone about his curate's indiscretion, and I do not believe that the late bishop would have dismissed Stringer because of it either. Vicars and bishops exercise discretion and dispense kindness: they don't threaten and bully. And there's another thing: there's no detail. Does he expect us to believe that he just happened to know about locking doors from the outside with the key on the inside?'

'So what are you saying, sir?'

'Well, I think that for a start we need confirmation of his story about Diana: my inclination is to believe that it happened only in his mind. Is it just a coincidence that the king's incest figures in the story of St Giles? But his letter has unloosed a curious idea that intrigues me: what if his story of the bishop's death is partly true?'

'Partly true? Which part?'

'Just so, which part! Could he have seen something or have his suspicions? His conscience plagues him not because he himself killed the bishop but because he had thought of killing the bishop! What it is to have such a tender conscience! Just imagine this. He has heard that the bishop is on the point of dismissing him, and he is deeply disturbed: he doesn't know that the motivation for this new move comes from Mrs Wyndham-Brookes. He plans murder – how seriously it is impossible for us to say - but before he can carry out his plan, he learns of the evening visit of Messrs Wilkes and Crabtree. While poised for their departure, so that he can beard the bishop in his den at the first opportunity, he is surprised by the arrival of yet somebody else. He waits, hears noise and knows that a foul deed has been committed. He blames himself, such is his sensitivity to his own weak spots, as if he himself had carried out the act. We are going to engage in a little sleuthing – '

'Isn't that what we do all the time anyway, sir?'

'– and in the meantime I am withholding this letter from Mrs Stringer, since it might do more harm than good; its writer expected it to come to the police first, and a few hours' delay won't matter. While I go and see Mrs Stringer, will you chase up Stringer's old vicar in Lincoln and find out what you can?'

I conveyed to Mrs Stringer the sad news of her husband's felo de se, and I need not trouble you with a description of the anguished scene that ensued. The distraught woman eventually assumed mastery of herself and confessed that she had for long worried about her husband's mental balance. She could tell me nothing beyond the fact that Simon kept his problems to himself but that he had seemed particularly ill at ease recently. Had he come in very late on Thursday night? He had, but Mrs S had not checked the time and so couldn't be accurate. In any case, her husband not infrequently worked late, as he was a conscientious secretary, and she thought nothing of it. As I was leaving, a car drew up, and the archdeacon alighted.

'Good morning, inspector,' he said. 'A sorry business; very sad. How is Margery – Mrs Stringer?'

'Bearing up, I think, but it's going to be a very difficult time for her. Tell me, archdeacon, did you have any inkling that Simon Stringer might do away with himself?'

It was still drizzling, but we stood there in the open, our collars turned up.

'Well, between you and me, inspector, Simon wasn't really very stable most of the time: a nervous, restless sort of chap.'

'He seems to have blamed himself for the bishop's death. Could there be any truth in this, do you think?'

The archdeacon turned the idea over in his mind.

'Well, you know, inspector, I've been having second thoughts about the whole business. I originally wondered, as you know, whether the chaplain, who is also vicar general, had a hand in it, but now I'm not so sure. I don't like the fellow, but he probably hasn't the guts to perpetrate a murder. I think the bishop's death was an accident.'

'Then why was the door locked?'

'This is how I see it, inspector. Someone – anyone – had designs on something in the bishop's study. Having chosen a time when they thought they could work undisturbed, they go in to look for it, drawing the curtains if they were not already drawn and locking the door against the possibility of intrusion. Unfortunately they forget about the annexe door, and as they are contemplating their next move, or perhaps already engaged in riffling through the bishop's correspondence or files, the bishop, fresh from his late night orisons in the chapel, walks in and surprises the searcher. Perhaps they are known to each other. The bishop is aghast at such boldness and demands an explanation. An ugly scene ensues. The intruder, however, escapes through the annexe door, which the bishop promptly locks against further disturbance or even an act of aggression, and then, before he can telephone for assistance to apprehend the intruder in the castle – if it is an outsider - the bishop, in his agitation, trips on the carpet. And there you are: *finito.*'

'What has led you to this, er, reconstruction, archdeacon?'

'Well, it is fantastic to suspect any member of his lordship's household of murder; I was at fault in even imagining it was possible, but I was badly rattled by the event when you first spoke to me No one else could get into the castle at night; so it has to have been an accident, don't you agree?'

I did not, but, unable to think of a ready riposte, I thanked Mr Rolfe for his idea and left him to proceed with his visit.

On my return to the station, looking, I daresay, less than my usual well-groomed and handsome self, peering through wet spectacles and with rain-drops hanging off the end of my generous nose, Hewitt had come up trumps with his investigation into the incident at Skellingthorpe. He had identified the present whereabouts of Mr Tidsdale – not difficult when you have multiple *Crockford'ses* within a hand's reach – and asked him why Mr Stringer had left his parish in 1952. There was no secret or mystery about it. Stringer had approached him one day to express his regret that he was inadequate to the tasks of a curate in a busy parish: what did he, Tidsdale, advise? It was Tidsdale who suggested that Stringer consider an administrative job, and so it came about. Hewitt felt – rightly, I believe – that he should bring up the subject of Diana Stringer, without divulging the whole story, and Mr Tidsdale had no recollection whatever of a visit of his curate's sister to the parish. Stringer had days off, and it was then that he regularly visited his family; they did not come to him. Furthermore, he, Tidsdale, had had no occasion whatever to speak to Bishop Wyndham-Brookes about Stringer, either at the time or since. To the best of his knowledge he had never met Bishop Wyndham-Brookes. It looked, therefore, as if the Diana story was fantasy – wishful thinking, perhaps! – and that the rest of Stringer's fears were the product of paranoia. I did not know whether to be relieved or disappointed.

EIGHT

We now had several more leads to follow up. I thought we needed to be quite sure what the arrangement was for locking Hartlebury Castle if the bishop had evening visitors; and I was anxious to pursue the idea that Stringer might have been partner in a small plot on the bishop's life. Inquiry led us to the conclusion that Stringer had only one close friend – apart from his wife, that is – a certain Carson Heywood. We ran him to ground at his small detached house at Moseley, a somewhat strung-out hamlet to the north-east of Worcester. The weather had improved, at least to the extent of being dry, and Mr Heywood was in his garden digging over an area of his vegetable patch. His welcome could not be said to be enthusiastic, but he explained this by saying that he was struggling to come to terms with his friend's death and was reluctant to entertain company. Margery Stringer had telephoned him with the distressing news, but so far he had no details. I told him that we should not keep him long. To avoid taking his boots off (I presumed), he led us to a summerhouse where we could sit and converse a while.

Mr Heywood was a curious person to talk to, because his eyelids lifted only a little, and to make any sort of eye-contact he had to tilt his head back, which was a little disconcerting; I suppose one would get used to it. In age he was forty or thereabouts, well-built without being burly. Greying hair, close cropped, aged him (I thought). However, once we were seated, he seemed more amenable to discussion.

'Can you tell me any more about poor Simon's death?' he asked.

'I'm afraid I can't,' I replied. 'We know so little ourselves.'

'Did he leave no message behind?'

Unsure quite how much to reveal, I hesitated.

'He did: he left a letter for his wife, but I should not like to say much more about it until she has had a chance to read it for herself. It seems that some supposed misdemeanour in his younger days preyed on his mind and that the bishop's tragic death brought it back. So, you were close to him, Mr Heywood: did you see him at all after the discovery of the bishop's body yesterday morning?'

'I did: he came round yesterday afternoon, and he was in a bit of a state. He'd got hold of some book from the bishop's library and wanted to discuss some of the things in it. Actually, I don't think he wanted to discuss them: that was just his excuse. He really wanted me to reinforce them.'

'What was the book, may I ask?'

'It was a collection of *Golden Sayings* by a thirteenth-century Franciscan friar, Brother Giles.'

'You mean Saint Giles?'

'No, no, quite a different person: I don't think Brother Giles has ever been canonised.'

'Can you remember anything of what Simon said?'

'Oh, yes, we spent a long time looking at a few of the sayings, which he or I would scribble down in the margin of a newspaper.' At this, he rose, strode over to a dustbin, lifted the lid to remove a folded paper, brushed it down and returned to join us. 'Let me explain a bit, inspector,' he went on. 'Simon told me that the collection of a hundred-and-something sayings is divided into sections according to topic. Some of the topics didn't seem to interest him greatly, but he seemed fascinated by two sections in particular, "On Penance" and "On the Recollection of Death". One saying in each of these two sections seemed to rivet his attention once he'd found it. Here, this is the first one,' he said, twisting the paper round to hit on the right place:

> Blessed is the man who has sorrow for his sins, and weeps night and day, and will not be consoled in this world until he comes to where all the desires of his heart are fulfilled.

The other one is a little bit longer. A worldly man had come to visit Brother Giles, if I remember rightly, and in the course of conversation said that he wanted to live a long time and enjoy everything that the world had to offer. Brother Giles replied as follows – wait a minute: no, yes, here we are:

> If you should live for a thousand years and be lord of the whole world, what reward would you receive at your death from the flesh

76

which you have served? On the other hand, even if you live for only a short while and yet do what is right and keep yourself from evil, you will receive an inexhaustible reward in heaven.

So we talked about sorrow for sin, and how one could know when sorrow for sin was sincere and complete, and whether people like Judas Iscariot qualified for God's mercy. We talked about sins of the flesh, and whether they were as serious as other sins, and whether some were so serious as to cut one off from God. As we talked, Simon seemed to be declining into some sort of morbid fascination with various sexual sins, and he eventually turned back in the book to a section headed "On the Holy Fear of the Lord".

"What about this one?" he cried:

With what security can a man who has offended his God so gravely that he is worthy of death go into God's presence?

He scrawled it down here, but he seemed to be labouring under a great inner agitation. He then almost tore the book as he turned to another saying and scribbled it down to reinforce his emotion:

Masters, preachers and priests (he read out) who are keener to be praised and honoured than to draw souls to salvation stand in disfavour with God. They may return from this disfavour if they confess and watch themselves in future; but they may remain so long in this state that the gate of mercy may be closed on them and they are cast out beyond salvation.

Well, inspector and sergeant, I began to fear for his equilibrium: he was almost raving. So I told him very firmly to calm down, to say a prayer, and then to tell me quietly what was troubling him. He said it was so awful he couldn't say any more.'

'Did you have any idea what he might be talking about, Mr Heywood?'

'Well, I didn't like to press him, for fear of increasing his agitation, but I did wish to give him every opportunity to unburden his mind, so I talked a bit more about God's mercy, and only one sin being unforgivable – according to the New Testament – and that good people like Simon had every hope of living out their days in the light of the divine grace. He reached for the book again, flipped back to a section on 'Obedience and Its Utility' and read out something like this. Hold on a minute, gentlemen,' Mr Heywood said as he squinted along the margin of his newspaper. 'Yes, here it is:

The man who places his head under the yoke of obedience but afterwards withdraws his head on the pretext of following a path of greater perfection commits a sin of great pride.

I asked him what possible relevance this could have, and it was then that he confessed to having murdered Bishop Wyndham-Brookes.'

'What?' I said. 'Are you sure?'

'What do you mean, am I sure? Of course I'm sure. On the other hand, I took his words to be the ramblings of a deeply disturbed individual, and I have dismissed them as fantasy.'

'Could you tell us exactly what he said?'

'I'll do my best, inspector, but I urge you to give no credence whatever to his account. He began by saying that he had for some time been gravely disturbed in his conscience by a serious sin that had pursued him for twenty years. Last week he was summoned by his lordship for a heart-to-heart, in the course of which the bishop apparently suggested that Simon looked round for another appointment. Simon asked him disbelievingly why he should wish to do that, as he was perfectly happy and was confident of giving the bishop every satisfaction in his work. His lordship told him that it had recently come to his attention that Simon had grossly betrayed his trust as an ordained clergyman and could no longer continue in his employ. The devil entered into Simon's soul – I quote his very words, gentlemen – and he determined to silence the bishop once for all, so that his employment would be safe.'

'I see,' I said. 'Did he give you any details of the murder?'

'He did, but as I say, I'm quite sure it was all in his mind: Simon would be quite incapable of cold-blooded murder.'

'What was his story?'

'On Thursday night, after two late visitors had left the castle, Simon went into the bishop's study to plead with him one last time to reconsider his decision. The bishop was in a relaxed mood and did not seem to take him seriously. "Oh," he said, "you'll have no trouble in finding another billet: look on it as an opportunity to serve God elsewhere. I'll give you a good reference, don't you worry." Simon entreated his lordship to change his mind, but the bishop was apparently immovable; so he grabbed the poker from the hearth. Sensing violence, the bishop rose from his chair the better to defend himself, but Simon struck hard as his victim turned and before he was fully balanced, and the bishop crashed to the ground. Simon waited for a long while, fearful that the noise had roused the household, but, eventually concluding that no one had heard, he took steps to effect his escape. Realising immediately that members of the household would be prime suspects, he decided to set the scene up as a terrible accident. He had read somewhere about there being ways and means of locking a door from the outside leaving the key on the inside. He had even had a go at it himself. It did not take him long to engineer the scene to his satisfaction. He made his escape via his usual side door in the north wing and went home.'

'One thing puzzles me,' I commented. 'Yesterday morning, Mr Stringer was the first to draw our attention to the fact that the bishop never normally locked his door. Why would he do that? If he had said nothing, the accident scene he had set up would have been even more convincing. As it was, he alerted us to the possibility of murder.'

'He told me that that point troubled him. When you arrived promptly in response to his call to the police-station, he was desperate to distance himself from the action. His best resource, or so he convinced himself, was to profess complete bafflement about the bishop's death: he knew nothing, it was so unlike the bishop to lock his door, it was all a complete mystery, and so on. When you immediately latched on to *murder*, he realised he'd made a mistake but thought he'd carried off your initial interview with him without arousing suspicion.'

'Did he at all mention the presence on the bishop's desk of a valuable volume from the library?'

'Only to the extent of saying that he hadn't seen it there earlier in the day.'

'You are now talking as if you believe he *could* have committed the murder!'

'I know, inspector. One half of me refuses to believe it, while the other half, as I think of his frame of mind yesterday, almost persuades me that he is guilty. I really don't know what to believe!'

'May I ask, then, how well you knew Simon Stringer? You seem to be having no little difficulty in coming to a conclusion about what he was and was not capable of.'

'I know. Well, I've known Simon for a good many years. I first met him at theological college, where we were students together. As I became increasingly interested in philosophy, I left to pursue an alternative career, but we kept up. We had had two close years together, and I reckon I came to know him pretty well. There was always about him a sort of dreamlike or fantastic cast in which his own shortcomings took pride of place. Now I am not a sociable man myself, inspector, and he and I forged a friendship built partly on loneliness and partly on the recognition of a kindred soul. So I recognised the symptoms. For most dreamers, exploits of derring-do and acknowledged heroism fill one's daydreams, but for others – those imbued with a sense of their own unworthiness - it is one's failings which occupy the mind, distorting reality so that everything that happens is always one's own fault. It is a downward spiral. Simon had a melancholy turn of mind at the best of times, although if he could be persuaded to forget his problems – which were mostly imaginary, I should think – he could be good company. He was quite widely read, he knew a lot about religion, he was interested in politics, history and music, and so on. His wife is often ill, and I think that got him down, but that's no more than most of us have to bear. But to return to your question, inspector: of course I can't be *certain* he made up his role in the bishop's death, but I think that, all things considered, I should be very surprised if it had happened as he said: unless, of course, I underestimate his sense of failure after the bishop's little chat with him.'

After our conversation with Carson Heywood, Hewitt and I returned to the station for a consultation over a warming and soothing pot of tea. A little less than twenty-four hours had elapsed since we last put our heads together, but I felt that the day's events and interviews had produced, if possible, even further confusion in my mind.

'Right, young Hewitt,' I exclaimed, 'last night we discussed yesterday's information. We had interviewed all six members of the bishop's household, the diocesan chancellor and the two clergymen who had been with the bishop on the fatal Thursday evening. Our conclusion was one big question mark: who, how, why and when? Have we learnt anything useful today?'

'Today, sir, began with the discovery of Simon Stringer's body and his suicide note. We have since met his wife, the archdeacon and Mr Heywood, but the entire day really has been devoted to the bishop's secretary: did he or didn't he murder the bishop?'

'And what is your answer, sergeant?'

'Mr Stringer's letter is in the form of a confession, but you yourself, sir, cast doubt on its trustworthiness, mainly on the grounds that it painted an unrealistic picture of the Anglican clergy, or at least of the two clergy who had most to do with Mr Stringer. After your brief meeting with Mrs Stringer, you noted that she confirmed her husband's confession in two ways. Firstly, she admitted beginning to fear for his sanity, and secondly, she told you quite openly that he had returned home late on the Thursday night, although she couldn't say what "late" might mean. The archdeacon, on the other hand, buck teeth, broken nose, pallid cheeks and all, had quite another suggestion. Not only was Stringer not the murderer, there was no murderer at all. The bishop's death was a sad accident. The archdeacon has obviously thought about the matter, but I'm unpersuaded by what amounts to no more than a guess. And finally we listened to the doubts of Mr Stringer's closest and long-standing friend, our philosopher Mr Heywood.'

'Yes, yet more questions! Mr Heywood struck me as treading a fine line: he suspects Stringer is guilty of the bishop's murder, but he considers it a betrayal of their friendship to tell us so outright. The only thing is, if Stringer is guilty, I doubt whether we've got enough solid evidence to convince the DCI that the case is closed. We shall just have to persevere.'

NINE

First thing the following morning – I know, a Sunday: a policeman's work is never done! – we returned to Hartlebury Castle, after first making sure that at least the resident members of the household would be at home. I intended to ask whether others gave credence to Stringer's confession and to question the housekeeper about the locking of the castle at night. There being no answer to our first ring, after a decent interval Hewitt rang again, and the housekeeper, Mrs Wedlake, opened the door to us, wearing her apron.

'Excuse me, gentlemen, I don't know why the men didn't open up to you. Make your way to the bishop's study. Can't stop, I'm afraid: I'm in the middle of baking a cake,' and with that, she disappeared at a waddle across the great hall before we had a chance to speak with her. It could wait. We made our way through the salon, and what should greet our ears but the sound of voices raised in anger! The scene was, in its way, a comic one. The bishop's chaplain, Revd David Skyner, large and muscular and physically imposing, stood facing the thin, balding and physically weedy almoner, Revd Havelock Blake, in the middle of the bishop's study. They were both red in the face, with the effort, clearly, of shouting at their adversary. They turned to face us as we knocked and entered, and fell silent.

'I hope we're not intruding,' I said lamely.

'No,' the chaplain said, 'you've come at just the right time. You can arrest this – this murderer and cart him off to gaol. The man's a disgrace to his profession.'

As the almoner opened his mouth to protest, or perhaps to renew their exchange of abuse, I intervened.

'Gentlemen, shouting like this is unseemly, in the bishop's very study, and I beg you to calm down. Perhaps it would be best if we spoke to each of you in turn?'

With a final glower at his opponent, Blake said, 'I shall be in my office when you're ready, inspector,' turned on his heel and disappeared into the salon.

For a moment Skyner stood still then seemed to recover himself.

'I'm sorry about that, inspector, sergeant. Do sit down. What can I do for you?'

'Your, um, difference of opinion with Mr Blake clearly concerns the bishop's death. May I ask how?'

'Yes, inspector, you may ask, and it will be a pleasure to tell you.' He pounded a fist into the palm of his other hand. 'That little runt thinks he's going to get away with it, but he won't if I have anything to do with it. These Bible-bashers make me sick!'

'Would it be advisable for you to start at the beginning, Mr Skyner? When we last met, you said you suspected the almoner of wishing the bishop dead, but the only reason you gave was that he had designs on Mrs Wyndham-Brookes' affections. Merely having a key to the castle and an office on the premises is not evidence of murder, you know.'

'Ah, but since then, other facts have come my way, inspector. I was just bringing them to the almoner's attention when you interrupted us.'

'Right, please tell us what you know.'

'Let me go back a bit. His lordship had confided in me that he wondered whether the problems facing the Church were not too much for him and that he should think of retiring. Naturally, I urged him against any such step: he was an influential member of the episcopacy, with a particularly crucial part to play in our rapprochement with Rome. He was a bulwark against liberalism in the Church. He had experience and learning on his side at a time of great difficulty. I had also come to believe that Mrs Wyndham-Brookes was getting impatient with her husband's seeming unwillingness to capitalise on his position as a prominent bishop: just when he was placed to rival the two archbishops in their leadership of the Church, he thinks of resigning and growing cabbages! Mrs Wyndham-Brookes is not every man's ideal of womanhood, but I hated to see her snubbed, frustrated and disappointed. I was also anxious, of course, to protect her from any machinations on the part of that insignificant almoner.

'Now on Thursday night, the night of his lordship's death, I was returning to my room, having collected a few things from the kitchen for a bit of supper, when I noticed, from my vantage point on the stairs, the almoner coming in by the side door. No reason why he shouldn't, of course, and I paid his entry no particular attention. I had my supper, read for a while, and then retired to bed. However, I couldn't sleep, so I decided to stand at the window for a bit. The day before had been a full moon. That Thursday, therefore, the moon had only just begun to wane, and I rejoiced in the view of the Worcestershire landscape from my window bathed in the moon's brilliance. As I stood there, the almoner came out of the side door of the castle, went to his car and drove off. Nothing peculiar in that. I noticed that the time was a little after midnight. However, as he hurried towards his car, he dipped his hand into his left jacket pocket, obviously replacing some item, transferred his bunch of keys from his right hand to his left to open the car-door with a free hand, got in and drove off.'

'Just a minute, Mr Skyner. Could you just go over that sequence again, with a little more explanation. I want to be sure I see what you're getting at.'

'Certainly, inspector. The man was walking away from me. His left hand dipped into his jacket pocket, and then immediately his right hand crossed the front of his body, the two hands disappeared from my view, and then his right hand re-emerged, empty, to grasp the door handle. By this time he was side-on to me, preparing to enter his car, which was parked with its rear into the car-park. There can be only one explanation for this manoeuvre. There was something in the man's left hand which was an encumbrance. He put this object into his pocket so that his left hand would be free to receive the bunch of keys from his right hand – the keys he had just used to lock the side-door of the castle. His right hand was then free to open the car-door, swinging it to his right, towards the engine.'

'Right,' I said, 'please continue.'

'Well, I gave none of this particular attention. I presumed that the almoner had been working on something in his office and was on his way home after a late night's work. Nothing peculiar struck me the following morning. I did not ask myself particularly how you came to the conclusion that the bishop's death was not an accident but murder: I was much keener on thinking about who on earth would wish to murder the bishop. However, this morning, as I was working on the arrangements for the funeral, I glanced up idly, thinking about who should preach the sermon, when the study-key on its peg by the door caught my eye. I was quite certain, at the back of my mind, that there were always two keys in that position; now there was only one. So I went back over the events of the bishop's death. When you first saw me, that Friday morning, you said merely that you suspected a member of the household of being responsible for the bishop's death, but I never thought to ask you why, and I realised that I had not been thinking straight or in a focussed manner. When we entered this study that Friday morning, both doors and the window were locked. A little later that morning, you asked me whom I suspected, if I were obliged to name a member of the household. Now, thinking back this morning to all that, I came to realise that the study-door leading into the salon must have been locked by the murderer using one of the two keys that habitually hung inside the door. That implied someone with knowledge of the study and a pre-formed plan for making it look as if the bishop had himself locked the door on the inside: it's not a gambit that would occur to you by accident or on the spur of the moment. I have no idea how it was done, and, as I say, I had not focussed on the problem, content that you had come to your own conclusions on the subject.

'As I sat here this morning, therefore, pondering this circumstance, I recalled the almoner's furtive movements on the night of the bishop's death. Well, perhaps "furtive" isn't the right word: his juggling of keys, then. The explanation leaped at me: what I had seen from my window was Blake with his left hand pocketing the study-door key that he had minutes before used to set up his accident scene.'

'Can I just interrupt you there, Mr Skyner?' This was Hewitt – to his credit! 'If Mr Blake had indeed come from the study, as you suggest, he would have had to walk across the salon and main hall and out through the north wing. That gave him ample time to pocket the study key. Why wait until he was outside, on his way to his car?'

'Perhaps he was in such a hurry he didn't think about it. Or perhaps he couldn't decide whether to hide the key on the premises or risk being caught with it on his person. Or perhaps he intended to plant it on someone else: the housekeeper, for example. How should I know?'

'And how,' I resumed, 'did your – conversation – with the almoner begin this morning?'

'As I sat here, with these thoughts seething in my mind, I determined to have it out with the man, and at that very moment he knocked on the door with a question about a particular charity – or some such trivial matter. Not long after that you arrived.'

'And he denied your accusation?'

'Of course: but he would, wouldn't he?'

'Now at the beginning of your conversation with us this morning, you made a rather dismissive reference to Bible-bashers, as if that had something to do with the matter. Could you explain?'

'Yes, inspector. I'm not sure how conversant you are with Anglican politics, but you probably know that between the extremes of the Church there is - how shall I put it? – a certain tension, or even antagonism. On the evangelical side this is fired by a sense of envy that we on the catholic wing are more powerful than they and by a consciousness that we have right on our side.'

'They are probably saying the same of you, Mr Skyner,' I said pacifically. He glowered.

'That is irrelevant, inspector. The crucial difference between us rests on the authority of the Bible. Evangelicals foster the absurd and untenable notion that the Bible dropped out of heaven ready-made, direct from the hand of God: it is inspired and inerrant, divine in both content and form. This attitude leads to fundamentalism, one of the most dangerous attitudes in religion, in my view. You see, it does not enable you to bring the light of intelligence and reason to bear on any item of religion: the answer is always, Oh, but it says in the Bible ... as if that were the last word on the matter.'

'How does that concern our present problem, sir?' Hewitt piped up again. The chaplain turned his head slightly to face him.

'Sergeant, if you refuse to use your reason, you are closed to all argument: only emotion can have any influence, and emotion without reason is a blind force. One of the most ridiculous sentiments ever to come from the pen of Matthew Arnold is his contention that "the true meaning of religion is not simply morality, but morality touched by emotion". It is nonsense, I needn't tell you. Religion has to do with our minds and wills, not with our emotions: we know, and we act accordingly. Feeling is for children: for those incapable of exercising mature judgement. If you are evangelical, you have no tradition of using your mind and every incentive to respond to events with emotion and "warm feeling". Blake is typical of his kind, I'm afraid.'

For a few moments there was silence.

'Have you anything further to add, Mr Skyner?' I asked eventually.

'No, inspector: is that not enough?'

My projected question about Stringer's declaration of guilt seeming otiose in the light of this narrative and then the forceful denunciation of the evangelical tradition of the Anglican communion, I forbore to ask it!

Hewitt and I left the study in search of the almoner. I felt quite sorry for the poor man after his mauling at the hands of the chaplain! It was time we righted the balance, if it could be righted. We ran him to ground in a species of broom-cupboard squeezed in between the kitchen and a toilet, to find him scribbling away industriously. Since there was not room for the three of us, he invited us to go along to the great hall and talk there. His sparse hair had not been recently combed – or washed! – and his narrow, emaciated features were not endearing. I dismissed these thoughts as secondary considerations. Once settled, I considered that there was no point, after the scene we had witnessed earlier, in beating about the bush.

'Mr Skyner tells us,' I said bluntly, 'that he has accused you of the murder of Bishop Wyndham-Brookes. May we ask whether you defended yourself?'

'Huh, that jumped-up, pretentious, windy snob: he doesn't frighten me! Just because he's clever, he thinks he knows it all. Yes, of course I defended myself, inspector: I had nothing to do with it.'

'But you were on the premises that Thursday night.'

'Yes, I had every right to be!'

'Would you like to tell us exactly what you did?'

'There's nothing to tell. I came, did my work and then went away again, that's it.'

'Please give us a little more detail, sir. You never know, you may have seen something relevant to our inquiry.'

'Oh, I don't think so, inspector, but yes, I can say a little more. Because of the St Giles' banquet, as I may call it, on the Thursday, I stayed for lunch, at the bishop's kind invitation. I'm invited every year, and I enjoy the occasion. Of course, while celebrating saints is acceptable, praying to them is not, but the opportunity to invite some disabled people to lunch with the bishop on St Giles' Day – you see, such invitations fall to me to issue – makes the whole thing worthwhile – for me, I mean. I didn't feel too good afterwards – perhaps I was a little immoderate in my consumption of preprandial sherry! – so I went home intending to return later in the day to complete some research on a charity I had not before heard of, and to do one or two other little jobs concerning a long-term project in Africa that we are sponsoring. In the event it was already quite late in the evening when I made my way back to Hartlebury. You see, as I live on my own, I come and go much as I please, with due regard, of course, for my parish duties. You may know,' he added with no little pride in his voice, 'that I double up as vicar of All Saints at Malvern Wells.'

'Yes, please go on, Mr Blake,' I said encouragingly.

'Well, I suppose I arrived at about nine o'clock – long after it was dark, anyway – and from the presence of a couple of cars at the front door, I deduced that the bishop had visitors. That didn't bother me: my work didn't require me to speak to his lordship that evening. So I made myself a cup of tea in the kitchen and then settled down in my office to complete the work.'

'Did you hear or see anybody else?'

'Yes, once or twice I heard people go in and out of the kitchen, but that's perfectly normal, even in the evening. So at about midnight – I'm guessing, really, inspector, but it *felt* like midnight! – I left to return home. I locked the side door – '

'I'm sorry to interrupt you there, Mr Blake,' I said, 'but please give us every detail you can remember. Mr Skyner is making some claims about your movements at this point.'

'I know, the silly fool is making out he saw me with the study key, having bashed the bishop over the head with his own poker. I shouldn't be at all surprised if he'd done it himself and then picked on me as a scapegoat. So I can tell you exactly what I did. I am right-handed, inspector. I opened the side-door, exited, and then turned back to check that it was firmly closed and had locked itself. I walked across to my car, which was on the far side of the car-park, feeling with my left hand in my left-hand jacket pocket to check that I had remembered to pick up my fountain-pen. I then transferred my bunch of keys from my right hand to my left hand, opened the car door with my right hand and got in. There's not the slightest mystery, inspector.'

'Did you hear or see anybody else at this point?'

'No, not a thing. There was a full moon, or as near full as makes no difference, and I paused for a moment to admire the castle and its grounds bathed in moonlight. Everything was extremely peaceful: nothing stirred.'

'Mr Skyner seems to think that you might be guilty because you are an evangelical. What would you say to that?'

'He talks nonsense, that Skyner! Just because he's not working class and regards himself as a highchurch theologian, he thinks he can look down his nose at the rest of us. Let me tell you something, inspector.' At this point the almoner leaned forward and adopted a more animated style than we had so far witnessed. 'Look at what Anglo-Catholics get worked up about: women priests, heresy trials, ecumenism, styles of worship, the colour of liturgical vestments – all Churchy things, absolutely nothing to do with bringing the Lord Jesus to the world! By their fruits ye shall know them. Now evangelicals haven't got a monopoly on charity and good works – of course not - but by the Lord Jesus we try harder! High Church is all bluster and fluster: words, and yet more words; technical theological jargon, way above people's heads, and nothing whatever to do with feeding the hungry and clothing the naked. That's what Christianity is about, inspector: not belief but fruits. So that young fool Skyner can say what he likes, my conscience is clear.' He paused and sat back in his chair, looking a little flushed. After a little while, I put him another question.

'When we saw you on Friday morning, Mr Blake, you wondered whether Mrs Wedlake might not have had a hand in the bishop's death. From what you have just said, you seem no longer to stand by that.'

'Inspector, sergeant, I have every regard for Mrs Wedlake, but she rather tires me with her attentions. I can speak frankly, I take it? She's lonely, poor woman, and because I'm single, she thinks we can make a go of it. I have no interest, and because of that I believe I can take a dispassionate view of the situation in her regard. I knew, from my conversations with his lordship in my official capacity as episcopal almoner' – I leave you, dear reader, to imagine the smugness with which this phrase rolled off Mr Blake's tongue! – 'that the housekeeper's position was precarious. Mrs Wedlake had been told this, and she had taken the news desperately hard. As one who lives on the premises, she has every opportunity to murder the bishop if the mood should so take her: more or less as and when she pleases! I really have only one thing to add to that, inspector. In the few days since – since it happened, I have noticed that she seems much relieved, no doubt believing that her future at Hartlebury is now secure. You can't blame her for that, can you? Likewise, Skyner lives in, and he too has every opportunity for murder. Perhaps the St Giles' lunch, with its reminder that the saint was content to retire into obscurity, prompted him to act in punishment for the bishop's shilly-shallying; but now I've let my tongue carry me away, when I should be speaking charitably of all, even the most toffee-nosed, pompous and self-regarding! Forgive me, inspector.'

Before we left the castle, and having ascertained that the bishop's relict would not be back home until the afternoon, we took the opportunity of having a quick word with Mrs Wedlake in her kitchen. I let Sergeant Hewitt do the talking: he was good at sweet-talking the women.

'Mrs Wedlake,' he began in his most ingratiating manner, 'we're sorry to trouble you again, but we'd like a bit of information, if you don't mind. Thirty seconds of your time?' She visibly melted in the warmth of his tone, although I suspected that Hewitt was alert to any mistake the widow might make that would incriminate her. Policing makes cynics of us all.

'Ask away, sergeant, it'll be a pleasure.'

'You usually lock the castle up at night?'

'Yes. If I'm away, the chaplain does it.'

'And on occasions like last Thursday, when the bishop has late visitors, what happens?'

'The bishop takes it on himself: he can't expect anyone else to do it for him, can he?'

'And which doors do you normally lock?'

'There's really only two doors, sergeant.' She backed over to the cooker to adjust one of the rings. 'There's the front door, which only visitors use, generally. Then there's a side door in the north wing, which the entire household use.'

'And what other doors are there? You said "really" only two doors.'

'Well, there's a side door from the chapel into the garden – a fire-exit – and a back door from the annexe next to the bishop's study into the trees along the moat.'

'So if the bishop was murdered at about midnight, by a visitor from outside the castle, the front door would still be unlocked?'

'Yes, because the bishop, being dead, wouldn't have been able to lock it, would he?' She smiled up at him. She had taken a shine to Sergeant Hewitt.

TEN

On our way back to the city, Hewitt came up with an astounding thought.

'Do you know what I was thinking, sir, as Blake was denouncing highchurchmen in general and David Skyner in particular?'

'No, not until you tell me, sergeant.'

'This may sound outrageous, but I don't think we can dismiss it out of hand.'

'No, sergeant,' I said patiently, as I waited for further explanation, idly admiring the passing landscape. I had asked Hewitt to take the unclassified road (Lincomb Lane, for those of you familiar with the neighbourhood) through the wooded landscape, with the river close by on our right, from Astley Cross to Holt and then the A443.

'And you won't rebuke me for foolishness, will you, sir?'

'For crying out loud, Hewitt, just get on with it! The worst that can happen to you is a disciplinary hearing and dismissal from the force.'

'Very well, sir: what if Skyner and Blake are in it together?'

'Please explain,' I said, at once intrigued by my young colleague's thought processes at this juncture.

'This is what I propose. Skyner and Blake were expecting us. They see us roll up to the front door and begin to argue furiously – in make-believe. They deliberately let Mrs Wedlake answer the door, to give the impression of being engrossed in their argument. They then, in our interviews with them, denounce each other's churchmanship and social origins, subtly – oh, so subtly - shifting the blame for the bishop's death on to Stringer or perhaps Mrs Wedlake. It is all sand in our eyes, sir. Now we know for a fact that both men were on the premises when the bishop met his death. We know also that both men had reason to wish the bishop dead. What could be easier than for the two of them to set up the murder scene and then fake innocence?'

'Crikey, sergeant,' I commented, 'your mind is even more tortuous than mine! Where on earth do you dredge such notions up from? Are you quite sure *I* didn't commit the murder? Perhaps I'd better consult my lawyer straight away!'

'Now I know,' Hewitt continued, ignoring my outburst, 'that at first sight a friendship between an upper middle-class highchurchman and a working-class evangelical is unlikely, but they have been thrown together for some years as fellow-members of the bishop's household. They meet at lunch whenever the almoner is on the premises; perhaps they share a constitutional in the grounds afterwards. They get to recognise each other's gifts in different spheres, and a friendship grows. In the course of their exchanges, the bishop's state of mind crops up: the difficulties in the Church, the stresses in his marriage, his increasing fatigue and so forth. They both admit that the bishop's death, for reasons of their own, would be desirable – and there you are, a plot, hatched out in the vortex of catholic-meets-evangelical dialectic, ripe for Hegelian analysis!'

'Good heavens, sergeant, you will go far – as a contortionist, perhaps; but even if it's true, how are we going to prove it?'

'Ah, there you have me, sir: I must bow to your superior intellect.'

Do you, erudite reader, recall Swift's happy quatrain?

'Tis an old maxim in the schools,

That flattery's the food of fools;

Yet now and then your men of wit

Will condescend to take a bit.

I confess my weakness!

We returned to Hartlebury that afternoon to have a further word with Mrs Proudie – sorry, that should read Mrs Wyndham-Brookes. It was by this time a mild, late-summer day, with fleecy white clouds scudding across the sky under the impetus of a light breeze and with a fresh tang to the air. The sun having passed its zenith, the front of the castle was in shadow, but the overall picture was still delightful. The widow herself opened the door to us and invited us to take our seats in the great hall while she went to ask Mrs Wedlake to rustle up a pot of tea. On her return, I began our conversation with a discussion of the secretary's suicide and confession. There was no point in concealing the contents of Mr Stringer's note, which I outlined to her in the most general terms.

'Now Mrs Wyndham-Brookes,' I said easily, 'this note does not ring true, to my way of thinking, at several points, but the one that concerns us here is this: it doesn't seem likely to me that your husband would have used Stringer's worries about his past, whether they were well-founded or not, to invite him to look for another post. Do you know for certain whether this part of Simon Stringer's story is true?'

'Oh, inspector, now that Mr Stringer has done away with himself, I feel awful about having told you my doubts as to his suitability. I am not a malicious woman – at least, I like to think I'm not – and I now regret what I told the bishop.'

'And what did you tell the bishop?'

'That the secretary was a weasely and insignificant little shrimp who should be sent on his way.'

'What did your husband say to that?'

'He politely told me to let *him* manage the members of his staff, and that he was perfectly satisfied with Stringer as a secretary.'

'I see. So as far as you know, he never spoke to Mr Stringer about looking for another job?'

'As far as I know, he didn't; and I should hate to think now that if he did, it was because of me.'

'If it's any consolation to you, Mrs Wyndham-Brookes, I don't believe the bishop spoke to him in those terms either, and I also think that Mr Stringer's problems were of his own imagining, so please don't blame yourself for anything. Now, do you think Mr Stringer would actually be capable of carrying out your husband's murder, for whatever reason?'

'I really don't know what to think, inspector. If the bishop never mentioned the possibility of ending his employment, Stringer wouldn't have had any motive, would he?'

'Quite,' I said evenly. 'So if you're having second thoughts, what are they?'

'A bishop is ringed about with enemies, inspector: you must see that. I don't know what to think any longer. It could be anybody.'

'Yes, perhaps it could. So may I turn now to your own situation? How long had you been married, may I ask?'

'Thirty-five years, inspector.'

'And it must have given you considerable pride when your husband was chosen to be bishop of this prestigious see?'

'Well, yes and no, inspector.'

'Would you care to elaborate on that?'

'It's a long story, inspector, and I'm sure you have better things to do than listen to me reminiscing.'

'No, please, carry on.'

'If you insist, although I assure you it's of no interest. I was the youngest daughter of a baronet. We lived in a country mansion in Wiltshire, kept servants, entertained and were entertained and generally lived the life of gentry. My father, Sir Oliver Scrutton, sadly widowed after only seven years of marriage, was ambitious for his daughters – too ambitious, in my case. My eldest sister was married off to Lord Smeeton's son Thomas, and my other sister to Lord Cadwick's son Jamie. They seem reasonably happy in their marriages. That left me, and no one seemed anxious to have me: just not attractive enough, I suppose, or perhaps too waspish. Now one of my father's best friends was Sir Peregrine Neville, who lived here in Worcestershire, at Pendock Park in the very south of the county. They were always visiting each other, going off fishing together, taking part in hunts, that sort of thing. One day – it was a weekend, I think, although that's got nothing to do with it – other guests at Pendock Park were Sir Ramsey and Lady Wyndham-Brookes. My father told me later that, although Sir Ramsey was "only a knight", his son was unattached and just about good enough for a baronet's youngest daughter – in danger of being left on the shelf, I imagine he was thinking. The attraction was that this son, Giles, showed considerable promise as a young country curate, with potential to go higher. My father clearly had visions, even in those early days, of a bishop's crosier floating into his stately home, scattering blessings and spiritual munificence wherever it went.

'In due course, a meeting was arranged between young Dr* Giles Wyndham-Brookes and me, at Pendock Park. Again, it was a weekend, ostensibly devoted to country sports, but in reality stage-managed by my father and Sir Peregrine, for the sole purpose of hitching me to the young vicar they had, in their rosy vision of the future, lined up for me. It was made quite clear to me that my father was counting on the match. Now I adored my father. I was not worldly-wise, although well-educated and well-travelled, and I relied more on his judgement than on my own. I wanted desperately to please him, even though, as it transpired that weekend and as I discovered at greater length later, I thought Giles a bit of a wimp – no, a complete wimp: clever, devout, industrious, an exemplary curate, but in character – how shall I put it? – flaccid, unadventurous. Inspector, I never loved my husband. Do you know why we never had children? Because I wouldn't let him near me. We have never shared a bed: bedroom, yes, but not bed. I squared this with my conscience by arguing that the marriage was not of my making: I married to satisfy my father's ambitions for me. I was tired of Giles within weeks of the marriage. He was so, oh, I don't know, so conventional and unquestioning and orthodox and – and yes, flabby. I can see now why his parents were so anxious to promote the match! On his own he would never have managed it. So for thirty-five years I put up with him. He was a good man in his way: a kind husband, a thoughtful employer, a sensitive bishop, but his lack of energy just got on my nerves. How did it come about that he achieved preferment in the Church? A combination of brains, religious zeal and conformity – and possibly his (semi-)titled parentage - made him the ideal candidate for the various steps on his way to the see of Worcester: what is called a "safe pair of hands". I do not intend to disparage the powers that be: we're talking about the early '50s, inspector, when eligible candidates for empty sees did not grow on trees. The Church, like the country, was trying to re-establish the old order, to return to something like the stability of the inter-war years, and Giles Wyndham-Brookes seemed to fit the bill admirably. And I suppose that, in his way, Giles was not a bad bishop.'

'Forgive my asking, Mrs Wyndham-Brookes, but did you never contemplate a relationship outside your marriage?'

'That is a very personal and rather impertinent question, inspector, and I'm not sure I care to answer it.'

'Forgive me if I sounded inquisitive or insensitive. It's just that a thought has occurred to me. If anybody got wind of the lack of fulfilment in your marriage, could he have wished to liberate such an attractive prize as yourself in order to grasp it for himself?'

I spoke flattering but not entirely insincere words. I was beginning to warm to this woman.

'If you put it like that, inspector, I can say without undue modesty that there *is* someone who has expressed such intentions in my regard, but I can assure you that intentions would never have resulted in action. However – good heavens, yes! - you've put me in mind of an incident that occurred some years ago, and which I had succeeded in pushing to the back of my mind. It might just have a bearing on my husband's death. I wonder. This is what happened. When Giles and I got married, we lived at Martley, where Giles was a humble curate getting a name for himself as preacher and divine. The rector, James Hastings, naturally occupied the rectory, while we lived in a cottage in the centre of the village. Martley is not large: about 1000 inhabitants, but it has an interesting history and is situated in gently undulating countryside known for its glorious fruit orchards, brilliant with blossom in the spring, which I adored. When we had been there a short while, Giles and I were out walking one day – on Kingswood Common, I think, but it doesn't matter – when we were accosted by a young woman in her twenties: dressed in bright, if not gaudy, colours, hair flowing out, with a sort of wild look about her. Very pretty, she was, but her eyes were fierce, like those of a cat roused to anger.

"So, Giles," she exclaimed, "tracked you down at last! You couldn't hide from me for ever."

"I wasn't trying to hide from you, Adina. This is Sybil, my wife," he added, trying to introduce us. I say "trying", because she completely ignored both my hand stretched out in greeting and me.

"You're a disgrace to your profession, you are. Call yourself a man? A mouse, more like."

"Adina, please be sensible. The past is the past, and there is nothing to be gained by raking over it."

She spat at him, and he, naturally, recoiled. The spittle ran down his face. I didn't know what to say or do, I was so surprised by it all. To my astonishment, she drew a small gun out of her jeans pocket and waved it about. She then took aim and fired. Fortunately, the gun clearly wasn't loaded, but it gave me a fright. Adina then took off over the common into the nearest trees, and that was the last we saw of her. Naturally, I questioned my husband about this "appearance", and he explained that he and Adina had been engaged to be married, that he had broken it off because he became convinced that she was mentally unbalanced, and that they had subsequently parted company - not exactly amicably, but certainly without violence or threats of violence. He had no idea how or why she had followed him to Martley. Now that this business has come back to me, inspector, if she was and is unbalanced, who knows what horrors she might not perpetrate? On the other hand, I'm probably being fanciful, and I've no doubt it's entirely irrelevant.'

'Have you any plans for the future, Mrs Wyndham-Brookes?' I asked after a short pause, in as kindly a tone of voice as I could muster.

'No, none, inspector.' She became tearful. 'Cast off on the dung-heap of history as a has-been: shunted aside and forgotten. May God's will be done.' Her head fell on to her ample chest; and with that we rose, said our goodbyes and made our way out of the castle.

An unpleasant surprise awaited us. As we circled the front lawn, I, in the passenger seat, descried the castle housekeeper, the well-built Mrs Wedlake, to my left, swaying round the side of the north wing, gesticulating frantically in our direction. Hewitt immediately pulled up, and I alighted to make my way towards her over the grass.

'Inspector,' she managed to say, before putting her hand to her chest to catch her breath. After a few heavings and gaspings, she said, 'Thank goodness I've caught you. You must come quickly.' Without another word, she led us – Hewitt had by this time joined us – towards the building to the north of the north wing: clearly at one time, in the house's populous past, the stable-block, with accommodation for the carriages and horses on the ground floor and for ostlers and other staff on the first floor. Today the anarchic group of buildings, built at different times, forms a rough horse-shoe. The housekeeper made her slow way to the centre of the middle block, with us in her wake, entered and climbed the staircase, panting with the effort. After negotiating a corridor and some more stairs, she stood in front of a door, and with one hand to her mouth, she gestured us with the other to enter the room so indicated. We found the body of a woman, curled up on the floor. She was clothed in ankle-length boots, trousers, and a baggy, loud, woollen top. The woman's age was probably mid-fifties, and her face retained a handsome symmetry under a flowing shock of rich, brown hair. Beside her on the floor were a mauve glass plate and the small photo of a young man. I knew at once that this was Adina. How did I know? Let us just say, instinct.

Having telephoned for the usual police presence, I asked Mrs Wedlake for further details of the discovery. We were sitting in her kitchen, whither she had resorted to recover her composure. It was warm there, although the accommodation for human posteriors left something to be desired.

'I had run out of bleach,' Mrs Wedlake explained. 'I remembered that there was a box of the stuff in the stables, so I went over to fetch a bottle. The door of the room was jammed. I thought of going back to the main building to fetch one of the men, but then I knew I couldn't be bothered with all those stairs again, so I simply put a shoulder to the door and heaved. The door fell open at the second attempt, and I saw – well, what I saw. That's all I can tell you, inspector.'

'Do you know the woman?' I asked.

'No, never seen her before.'

'How might she have got in?'

'Easy. The building is left open all day: it's used by all sorts of people. Anyone can wander in: there's nothing of value in there.'

Our next and obvious task was to ask Mrs Wyndham-Brookes to identify the body before it was removed. She confirmed my suspicion, with the caveat that the passing of the years rendered her identification less than totally certain. I told her frankly that I could not believe that her story about Adina and the poor woman's presence on the premises were a coincidence.

'What are you driving at, inspector, if I may ask?' Her manner had, from being compliant, reverted to waspish.

'What I am getting at, Mrs Wyndham-Brookes, is that you knew Adina was at the castle, that her body would be found sooner or later, and that you mentioned the part she had played in your husband's life just to prepare us for the discovery. You spoke as if her memory had sprung up spontaneously, triggered by talk of your early married days, whereas all the time you were hiding knowledge, yes, Mrs Wyndham-Brookes, knowledge.' I said this with some vigour, determined to bounce the bishop's relict out of her complacency. I did not succeed.

'I resent the implications of what you say, inspector, and I reject categorically any accusation that I knew about Adina's body in the stables: you have my word as a Christian woman.' She drew her considerable frame up with an impressive show of dignity and then stalked out into the corridor. We heard her march majestically down the stairs and bang the stable-block door behind her in fury.

There were no marks on the body that we could discern. Our reconstruction thus far – which was not very far, I admit – was that Adina had entered the room, perhaps to hide, perhaps to wait, that the door had jammed and, unable to leave or attract attention, she had died of a heart attack. (It turned out that we were right about the cause of death; but an alternative explanation occurred to us later.)

Inquiries set in train by our police headquarters led us to a detached house in Bishop's Way(!), not far from the railway-station to the north-west of the centre of Andover, in Hampshire. There a bereaved Joel Colver received us. Colver was a man of sixty, rubicund in visage as of one familiar with the fruits of the vine, fleshy in build, not unhandsome in a rough sort of way. We learnt that he worked as manager of a restaurant in the city.

'I can tell you so little,' he assured us when we had given our news and confirmed his worst fears. He had reported his wife missing yesterday. 'Adina told me she was going to Worcester for a couple of days to look up Giles Wyndham-Brookes. He was an old flame of hers, for whom she retained some tenderness. I made no objection.'

'What plans had she made for accommodation?' Hewitt asked him.

'I don't know details: she said a hotel, but I don't know which one.'

'Do you know why she went at this particular time?' Hewitt persisted.

'No, although "blue moon" was mentioned as having something to do with it.'

'Can you remember exactly what she said, sir?'

'No, not really. Why, is it important?'

'We don't know yet sir, not until you tell us.'

'Adina dabbled in wicca, whatever that might be exactly, and she said that, according to the best authorities, the blue moon, and I think I can quote her very words here, "holds the knowledge of the goddess and therefore contains three-fold energy": all baloney, as far as I am concerned, but that's what she said. Myself, I'm not even sure what a blue moon is!'

ELEVEN

Hewitt and I embarked on an investigation into wicca in general and Adina Colver's interest in it in particular that occupied us for the rest of the day – and, if one includes our long interview with the dead woman's husband, half the night as well! I resume our findings for you, patient and busy reader. We put it all together with help from three sources: Joel Colver himself, the jumble of papers and books in his wife's desk, and expert knowledge from headquarters. My précis skills, learnt laboriously and painfully at school, came in handy!

The first thing we discovered was that Adina had been studying the life of Blessed Giles of Portugal, also known as Blessed Giles of Santarém, whose contemporary biography, by an anonymous writer, is, to modern scholars apparently, fantastical and therefore untrustworthy. (Adina's well-thumbed copy of a pamphlet titled *Blessed Giles of Portugal: A Life* by A Dominican Nun was full of her scribblings.) However, we are interested here not in fact but in legend! Let me fill you in briefly. Giles, the son of a wealthy and influential family from near Coimbra, born in the 1190s, studied theology and was destined for the priesthood. However, he preferred the science of medicine, and, with the intention of studying that discipline at Paris, he set off on foot through Spain, over the Pyrenees and up through France. However – so the story goes – falling in with a stranger, he was persuaded to stop off at Toledo and study the black arts instead. After seven years' study, he sealed a pact with the devil, signing it in his blood: he would give himself to Satan in exchange for knowledge and the power that comes with it. After seven years in Toledo, he moved on to Paris, studied medicine and practised as a doctor, but his conscience – or some supernatural power - got the better of him: a ghastly nocturnal vision alerted him to the dire state of his soul. He burned his magical books, smashed his phials and potions and set off to return to Portugal, a changed man. As he staggered on foot into Valencia, on Spain's eastern coast (had he not strayed a bit?), he was hospitably received by some Dominican friars, stayed and became a friar himself, repudiating his evil and wasted past and doing penance for his sins. Thereafter he filled various posts of importance in the Dominican Order, was favoured with the gifts of ecstasy and prophecy, and died in an odour of great sanctity in 1265, in his seventies. So much for the life of Blessed Giles (not yet canonised, but on his way!).

Adina seems to have been attracted to this life, legendary or not, by its promise of hidden knowledge followed, after due repentance, by holiness: one could have both! (I presume also that the man's name had something to do with it!) Quite why people believe that knowledge rather than appropriate behaviour brings salvation eludes me: this elitist view excludes, probably, 97% of humankind; but that is by the bye. Adina was influenced, by this holy man's experience, to dabble in wicca. Now wicca is an anthropologist's nightmare! As I came to understand it, wicca is a recent pagan religion which, for the most part, revives theories and practices of Greek and Roman mythologies, intermingled with generous dollops of other so-called religions: Scandinavian, Indian, Celtic and so forth. The reader will have detected incredulity in my words. Forgive me! I approached the matter with as much openness as I could, but I finally came to the conclusion that, apart from the laudable principle to avoid hurt, the whole thing is a quagmire of nonsense. However, that is not to our purpose. Let me outline for you the particular form of wicca which Adina espoused.

I have just used the words 'an anthropologist's nightmare' – advisedly. 'Wicca' seems to function as a blanket term for a huge number of beliefs, systems and rituals. Adina believed in a horned god, identified with the sun, Pan, the oak, the holly, the Green Man, and a goddess, identified with the moon, mother earth, the rowan etc. These two deities function in complementarity. Her desk contained a large number of drawings of these gods. Worship of the deities brings the power to influence events, and one procedure in particular is known as Drawing down the Moon: the devotee stands erect, arms stretched upwards with the palms towards the heavens, chants a hymn known as the Charge of the Goddess:

Listen to the words of the Great Mother:

Bow before my spirit bright,

Aphrodite, Arianhrod,

Lover of the hornéd god,

Queen of witchery and night etc.

enters a trance state and becomes the goddess's vehicle for prophetic
utterances and powerful happenings. Now I repeat that I have no idea how
other wiccans regard these ideas: I am relating only what Adina Colver
seems to have believed. In her desk was one spell in particular, either
contrived by herself or perhaps the gift of a priest or priestess. It was called
Spell for the Retrieval of a Lost Lover. The simple requirements were a
photograph of the beloved and a glass plate, purple in colour (on the
grounds, I presume, that purple is a combination of blue and red; blue
'harnesses the heavens to do your bidding', we read, while red symbolises
energy, courage, strength and so the goddess). The practitioner places the
photograph face down on the plate for fifteen minutes and then, adopting
the appropriate erect position, recites the following incantation:

Mother Goddess, Rowan Tree,

Bring my lover back to me.

Red for loving, red for death,

On my lover waft your breath.

I apologise for burdening you with these details, but we needed to know
what Adina was doing at Hartlebury, and I wish you to follow our
reasoning. Now this spell, we understood from her papers, is best recited (1)
on a Thursday, (2) at the time of a blue moon, (3) in the open air and (4)
preferably under an oak, this latter presumably to harness the god's power
as well. If the lover has not responded within twenty-four hours, the spell is
to be repeated. I was stunned by all this ritual. If people believe it works,
they are more gullible than I ever thought! However, I must not let my
personal prejudices (if that is what they are) lead me from the path of
impartial investigation.

Now the timing could not have been more propitious for Adina's
purposes, as we divined them. Here was a blue moon falling on a Thursday
– and how often does that happen? Let me explain briefly what we
discovered about blue moons. I was learning fast! There are at least four
meanings of 'blue moon', depending on the background from which you
approach the phrase (respectively, priest, farmer, wiccan, astronomer):

- the first full moon in the six weeks of Lent, if there should be more
  than one
- the 'extra' full moon in a season of the year if that season contains five
  and not the usual four

- the second full moon in a calendar (solar) month
- a literal blue moon when the full moon is turned a light shade of blue by the proximity of Venus or by some earthly phenomenon like the dust from a volcanic eruption.

It did not take us long to discover that wiccans in general, and Adina in particular, opted for the third meaning above. In wicca, a blue moon is particularly significant in the casting of spells, since it is an unusually good time to set specific goals. This is because 'it holds the knowledge of the goddess and therefore contains three-fold energy' (I quote from Adina's papers), and because 'it represents a time of heightened communication between our physical being and the Great Grand Mother Goddess'. How wiccans arrive at these conclusions I am afraid I cannot tell you!

Our reading of the situation was therefore this. Adina pines for her old flame, now a respected bishop in the Church of England. She determines to cast a spell to repossess him. Of course, she might have cast this spell on any number of previous occasions: on her and the wiccan understanding of 'blue moon', one occurs about every two and a half years. Perhaps she recited the spell every new moon, whether it was 'blue' or not; perhaps she recited it every morning on waking up; we were not destined to find out. Anyhow, she realises that the 31 August 1966 offers a peculiarly auspicious place and moment, because the day of the week, the phase of the moon and the presence of rowan and oak coincide in a rare manner. She sets off to cast her spell. She does so in the castle grounds under the blue moon of Wednesday 31 August. Twenty-four hours pass, and nothing happens. It is now Thursday night, late. The spell has apparently not worked: the bishop has not sent her word, has not emerged from his castle, has made no contact whatever. Did she cast the spell a second time? Or did she, in her desperation and frustration, enter the castle as she saw the bishop's visitors leave and stoop to murder?

I asked her husband what he could tell us about Adina's past life. I felt we could not make a reasoned judgement without knowing something about her. He kindly showed us some photos of his wife in her teens and since: an undoubtedly handsome woman, with an hour-glass of a figure, copious locks of a rich brown colour, full eyebrows neatly trimmed, high cheek-bones, more than a suggestion of red in her cheeks, generous lips. We came to understand also, however, that her physical attractiveness was marred by an uncertainty of temperament and a deep moodiness that some might call a psychopathology. (I do not call it a psychopathology, but only because I am not sufficiently well versed in the technicalities!) Adina

Fernihough-Smith was born in 1909, the second daughter of the Hon. Augustus Fernihough-Smith, an auctioneer and estate agent in the London borough of Putney. After a private education at a girls' school in Surrey, she went to a finishing school in Switzerland, where all manner of etiquette, image-management (or its equivalent in those far-off days!) and deportment was taught, as well as household practicalities, some music, some French and whatever else contributes to the creation of a well-bred young lady (like walking with books on her head and crossing legs endlessly until the movement is right). Her first job was as a secretary to the managing director of a large London hotel. When she tired of this, she took a similar situation at another London hotel, apparently believing that a change would bring into being a pool of exciting possibilities hitherto denied her. By now it was 1934, and Adina was beginning to worry that the man of her dreams was to elude her for ever. It was at this time, however, that she met and married an army captain called Sheridan Sawle. There were no children of this marriage, and Captain Sawle was killed in the first year of the war. Secretly she was content with this state of affairs, as she was not sure that marriage with Sheridan was quite the bliss she had once imagined it to be, and it was not long before she set out to find herself another mate. What she needed, she told herself, was not a masterful, gallant, graceful and confident youth in the mould of an army captain, but a biddable, easy-going, moneyed man of the world who would whirl her into the highlights and allow her to shine. It was her misfortune that she alighted on Mr Joel Colver, an overweight toper without the energy or acumen to set up a business of his own and only just on the right side of vulgarity. Happily, neither the Hon. Augustus nor his lady lived to see this decline in their daughter's fortunes. On the other hand, Adina, according to her husband at any rate, was more than content with her lot, except perhaps for the want of real affluence. Up to her death, Adina had been working as the manageress of the Hampshire golf-club near Andover.

It is always more difficult to describe a person's character than it is to outline her career. Even when one has enumerated the virtues and vices that co-exist, the whole eludes one. However, we gradually built up a reasonably coherent view of Adina, which I share with you. Of above average intelligence, she prospered at school, favouring the arts over the sciences (but then that is often the way where girls are concerned), but chose not to go on to university, on the grounds that finishing school had finished her schooling. She was a good needlewoman, a satisfactory cook, a tolerable pianist and a reasonable linguist. She was gregarious, enjoying the company of both men and women; she liked dancing, partying, holidaying with friends. She took an interest in politics but was not actively engaged except to the extent of casting her vote in elections: she would not have considered taking part in parades, processions, demonstrations, protests and the like. In religion, she had been raised as a practising Anglican, tending to the middle of the road. For her reading, she enjoyed a wide variety of novels, both classic and modern, some biography, some poetry, some drama, particularly Shakespeare, and some romance. (She rather despised *auto*biography as being the product of a self-absorbed personalities which led to an emphasis on the individual rather than on the wider implications for humanity in general.) Her musical tastes were equally eclectic, tending to the classical but not above more popular styles.

On the whole, therefore, Adina was an agreeable, extraverted, sociable, even-tempered being, but deep in her psyche were disturbing and irrational forces which might best be described, in strictly non-mythological and non-religious terms, as demons. Adina's demons led her to spasms of anger, depression, extravagant shopping, jealousy and excessive drinking. This is a volatile mixture which did not make her marriages easy for her husbands.

The question before us was whether this complex character was capable of the forethought and planning needed to murder the bishop. I put the question directly to her husband.

'Inspector,' he said, 'how do I know? Most of Adina's moods came and went in a flash: they flared up but as quickly subsided. Occasionally they could last a few days, but then she would emerge as if nothing were untoward. You're talking about a plan to leave an accident-scene behind her, which, if I understand you correctly, requires patient experimentation and a considerable degree of cool-headedness. I'm not sure Adina would be capable of that. She would be more likely to go for the weird and wonderful, the experimental, the off-beat, the intuitive, but I confess I really can't be certain. Casting spells left the outcome to hidden forces which perhaps rather excited her imagination as well as gave her confidence that she was not alone in her endeavours.'

'Mr Colver,' I asked him tentatively, 'would you say your marriage was a happy one?'

'I'm not sure I see the relevance of that question, inspector, and I'm not sure I care to answer it.'

'Please don't take offence, sir. I'm thinking about why Adina seems to have wanted to regain the bishop's affections, if that is what she was indeed doing at Hartlebury.'

'Yes, I see. I apologise if I seemed a little abrupt. In my mind there is no question that Adina loved me, just as I loved her. We were not really similar in temperament, but we gelled; I can't explain that rationally: there was a chemical magic at work. On the other hand, Adina's mind was not always – how shall I put it? – on the job. She could go off at a tangent, for no apparent reason, and she could be completely immune to logical argument. In that sense she wasn't an easy person to live with. But yes, we were happily married, inspector, as much as any other couple I know.'

Here he paused. I found myself wondering how the attractive and vivacious Adina had settled for this rather humdrum and unexciting individual. My thoughts were cut short when he resumed.

'I'm not a psychologist, inspector, but can I tell you how I see things? Adina bitterly regretted her father's death in 1937, and she has been looking round ever since for a second father. She became fixated on the Bishop of Worcester, not principally because she had known him in her early womanhood, but because he had assumed the mantle of a father-figure in the Church. She was fascinated by the episcopal vestments and attendant paraphernalia: the flowing robes, the crosier of the leader and shepherd, the mitre of authority. I think she researched ways of bringing him back into her life, and since society would have opposed overt attempts, she resorted to wicca.'

'And when that didn't work,' Hewitt interrupted, 'she murdered him!'

Colver became quite angry.

'You've no right to say that, sergeant. You have no evidence: you've jumped to an unwarranted conclusion.'

'Yes, sir, sorry, sir,' Hewitt said apologetically. 'My thoughts were running ahead of me.'

It seeming doubtful whether our interview with Joel Colver would yield anything further that was useful, we left to undertake the 85-mile drive back to Worcester. It was late at night, quite dark, but the roads were quiet. It had begun to rain. I asked Hewitt for his reactions to the day's events: our return to Hartlebury in the early morning, the apparent argument between the chaplain and the almoner, our brief conversation with Mrs Wedlake, the discovery of Adina's body, our research into wicca and our long interview with the widower. (It had been quite a long day altogether!) Hewitt's youthful profile showed up against the lights of oncoming traffic , such as it was, as he stared ahead in concentration on the road.

'Well, sir, may I apologise first of all for my outburst back there? It won't happen again.'

'A very mild lapsus, sergeant, completely understandable. I share with you your frustration at not getting to grips with this murder: the bishop's been dead three days, and we haven't fingered anybody, or even come near it!'

'One thing we haven't really talked about, sir, is the connection, if any, between Mrs Wyndham-Brookes and Adina Colver. Mrs W-B gave her word as a Christian woman that she was unaware that Adina's body was on the premises, but there was a great deal she didn't give her word on. For example, she didn't specifically deny that she was aware of a plot on Adina's part to do away with the bishop or even that Adina had murdered of the bishop. She could have been privy to both facts and yet still assured us that she didn't know that Adina had died in the stables instead of making good her escape. I'm sorry to be suggesting another collusion, sir, but is it possible that Mrs W-B and Adina were in cahoots? What would be your views on that, sir, if I may ask?'

I gave the matter some thought.

'Well,' I said after ruminating, 'you might have hit on something, but we should need a good deal more proof that Mrs W-B and Adina still knew each other after all these years and that they had met recently – I presume recently – to put the finishing touches to a scheme to polish off the bishop. My instinct is that Adina's interests lay not in murdering the bishop but in getting him back off his wife. Her own marriage may not have weighed very heavily with her, despite Colver's protestations to the contrary. Oh, I don't know, sergeant, I'm flummoxed!'

Hewitt said nothing, so after a minute or two I continued.

'And that's the third holy Giles we've come across in three days! I wonder how many more we are destined to meet.'

We had not long to wait before finding out.

TWELVE

The village of Lorenzana in the Apennines of the Neapolitan hinterland, is, I regret to inform you if you do not know it, rather non-descript. Its 2000 inhabitants have built themselves red-roofed houses clustered on a south-facing slope, some 700 feet up, sliding down to a bridge over the river that runs along the bottom of the hill. Only one building claims the aesthete's attention, the so-called Roselli baronial mansion, but in truth it is, while quite fine in its way, modest. The church, dedicated to Maria Santissima della Sanità – a relatively rare appellation for the Madonna, I think – does not measure up to its namesake in Naples thirty miles away, which is an opulent basilica. A small Franciscan friary, constructed in the fourteenth century when the village was tiny, is little more now than a few low walls in the garden of a village house. However, the friary's most famous son lives on the name of the street in which the ruins reside: vicolo Beato Egidio.

An inhabitant of Lorenzana, one Salvatore Scifo, was in Naples for the day. The inhabitant of Lorenzana who wishes to visit Naples walks or cycles down to Castelvenere, three miles distant, catches a bus to Benevento, fifteen miles distant, and then boards another bus for Naples. Half the day is already gone! Salvatore is on a mission: he wishes to trace a relic of Beato Egidio which he believes was stolen from the church of Maria Santissima in 1923. His knowledge is sketchy. According to his great-grandmother, who had been born and spent her whole life in the village, the last friars finally left Lorenzana in 1818, when she was eight, taking the relics with them to more commodious premises further to the west, where a larger population could support the growing number of mendicant friars wishing to join the community. By way of gratitude to the village which had harboured them for five centuries, they donated to the parish church a finger of Beato Egidio, supposedly removed from the body six years after the blessed's death in 1518, when, again supposedly, the body was found incorrupt. This finger was housed in a bejewelled reliquary in which sat a window, enabling the faithful to reverence it in their prayers with eyes delighting in the physical sight of the (by now slightly wrinkled) finger. In the best traditions of nineteenth-century Italian piety, the finger was accorded miraculous powers in the specific area of animal welfare. It is that that prompted Salvatore to embark on his quest. According to his great-grandmother, her father's flock of sheep had been threatened with an outbreak of brucellosis that risked destroying their viability, and with them his livelihood. It was to the powers of the Blessed Egidio's finger that he owed the salvation of his flock. The old lady therefore laid on her great-grandson the imperative task of returning the relic to the village: he owed it to his ancestors. Let me explain further: please be patient!

Egidio, born in 1443, was the son of a local farm labourer. As he grew into early manhood, his piety led him to withdraw into the hills to live a solitary life as a hermit, where his daily companions were the fauna of the mountainside: the marsicano bear, the chamois, the wolf and the wild boar; the peregrine, the eagle, the chough, redstarts, woodpeckers and Bonelli's warblers; the yellow-bellied toad and the Orsini viper; and so forth! He lived off berries and wild fruits, fungi, edible roots, wild herbs. In due course his life-style attracted the curious and the sensation-seeking, and he moved back down the hill to work on an isolated farm as a labourer. Naturally, this refuge was no more secure than his previous habitat, and eventually he joined the Franciscan friars at Lorenzana, where his new brothers afforded some protection. There he died in 1518, in the seventy-sixth year of his age, full of holiness and prayer. His fame lived on: ecstasies, miracles worked for sick animals, prophetic utterances – and above all, levitation.

Do you believe in levitation? On the one hand, stories of it abound in history. On the other, it is hard for a twentieth-century rationalist to credit. It has been studied and three forms identified (bear with me!): ecstatic ascension, ecstatic flight and ecstatic stride. Practitioners include – are said to include! – St Paul of the Cross, St Philip Neri, St Stephen of Hungary, St Peter of Alcantara, St Francis Xavier and above all the seventeenth-century Italian saint Joseph of Cupertino (referred to by the English-speaking irreverent brigade as Cup-o'tea-now), who regularly soared into the air, attained considerable heights, and stayed aloft for long periods of time. Various naturalistic explanations have been advanced, but they do not satisfy everyone. The religious person will accept levitation as evidence of the power of the Divinity over the earth-bound human body.

It was no wonder that the villagers of Lorenzana were grateful for the gift of a finger of this local son. They commissioned a fitting reliquary, which was placed safely in a side-chapel of the parish church. There the faithful venerated the memory of Egidio, prayed for their sick animals and for the gifts of simplicity, humility and holiness, and rendered thanks to God for living so close to one who had received the divine favour. On the night of 11-12 January 1923, at the height of a storm, the church was broken into and the reliquary prised from its stand and stolen. Nothing had been heard of it since, despite desperate and fervent appeals by the villagers for the return of their talisman. Salvatore reasoned as follows. If the relic was stolen by someone wishing to possess a miraculous object, there was probably no hope of its recovery: it would be secreted in some humble house or ducal castle or private chapel to bring benefits to the household. If, on the other hand, it had been stolen for the monetary value of the reliquary, there was every chance of its being sold on, perhaps piecemeal, perhaps as a whole. Salvatore thought that this latter possibility was worth exploring. He reasoned further that, the village of Lorenzana being somewhat remote, the perpetrator of the theft was a person with local knowledge whose first port of call would be an antiquarian shop in Naples, rather than some superior premises in the capital. He therefore called in turn on all antiquarians in the Bay of Naples, hoping to strike lucky. He found nine dealing in one way or another with antiques. At each he inquired after the reliquary, describing its contents, showing a photograph and outlining its importance to the local community. This was a bad mistake, because the dealers immediately, and rightly, concluded that the artefact had been stolen, and they were unlikely to take the risk of being known to deal in stolen goods. He therefore returned home and decided to wait for a year.

At the expiry of that period, he returned to Naples, this time dressed as a priest, and inquired round the same shops for a suitable relic to put in his new church – preferably the relic of a Neapolitan saint. This time he was lucky – in a sense. One antique-dealer told him that he was just too late: a tourist had visited his premises a week or two before and bought an example that would have suited him admirably! Yes, it was a genuine relic, a finger, authenticated by a piece of paper adhering to the inside of the rear casing and guaranteed to come from the hand of a Franciscan friar who had died locally some centuries before, in an odour of the greatest sanctity and with an almost unparalleled reputation for miraculous doings. This was a profound blow, but it reassured Salvatore that the reliquary was still intact. He inquired closely of the proprietor of the premises concerning the identity and provenance of this tourist. The information he received in response to his inquiries was meagre. The buyer was English – he thought; reasonably well-off, a *gentiluomo*, perhaps – he thought; and he was acquiring the relic as a quaint souvenir of his holiday in Italy. The only identifying feature he could remember was gold initials stamped on the side of the buyer's leather wallet as he paid for the reliquary: GWB. He remembered because they were the initials of a German association for the assistance of the handicapped, *Genossenschaft Werktätiger Behinderter,* which had just opened offices in Naples, and his eldest daughter was one of the first beneficiaries.

It transpired that Salvatore had neither the financial means nor the time to undertake a trip to London: he was a son of the soil who knew that a search for the reliquary was beyond him. Visiting Naples for a day was within his capabilities, but a trip to London – and perhaps New York and Brisbane and goodness knows where else - and a stay of weeks or even months was out of the question. Only too aware of his great-grandmother's injunction, he commissioned his eldest son, also Salvatore but known to his family and friends as Toti, to shoulder the responsibility if ever his means should so permit. If this should not prove possible, he must instruct *his* son likewise, until such time as the honour due to Beato Egidio's finger should be satisfied. It turned out, therefore, that it was only in the summer of 1963 that Salvatore Scifo Junior felt able to carry out his instructions. He realised that his quest was going to be extremely difficult. Searching for an English-speaking gentleman with the initials GWB, in a nation of fifty million people – if, indeed, he was British at all, and not a New Zealander or a Canadian, an American or an Australian - was an extremely tall order. Toti was below average height but broad, with a drooping moustache and dark brown hair, a shambling gait and a wide grin. He had inherited from his forebears the Italian concept of family honour as well as the quiet perseverance that comes from working the soil. Toti knew no English, and some would have considered that a devastating handicap, but he was not daunted. Having secured lodgings in London, he sought advice at a public library as to where he might begin his search. He was pointed in the direction of the nation's telephone directories. He was also advised about the existence of other citizens' lists: the electoral roll, the honours' list, local directories and so forth, but none of them seemed designed to meet his requirements easily. Realising that this was probably not the best approach, he visited the Italian Embassy in the West End. The official who spoke to him, with scant patience, he thought, probably on the grounds that it was what he called a *ricerca inutile* but which sounded so much more vivid in English as a wild-goose chase, suggested placing advertisements in the national press, and perhaps also in one or two of the more widely read provincial newspapers.

Armed with this new suggestion, Toti returned to the library. Thinking to save his costs, he excluded newspapers that were unlikely to be the reading material of *gentiluomini* and therefore concentrated on the broadsheets: the *Times,* the *Guardian,* the *Telegraph,* the *Scotsman,* the *Financial Times.* He could always extend his search later if it should prove necessary. After consulting the library staff, he drew up the following advertisement:

> Italian historian researching Neapolitan saints' relics anxious to contact Mr GWB concerning small jewelled reliquary from Lorenzana purchased in Naples in 1923. Please reply Box. No. etc.

To his delight, this advertisement received a response:

> Sir, If you care to make an appointment with my secretary, on [such-and-such a telephone number], I may be able to help you in your research. GWB.

It transpired, therefore, that on Thursday 20 June 1963, il Signor Scifo Salvatore called on Bishop Giles Wyndham-Brookes at Hartlebury Castle in connection with a silver reliquary containing the finger of Blessed Giles of Lorenzana. Now this visit occurred shortly after Revd Simon Stringer took up his appointment as his lordship's secretary, and it seems that the secretary was the only witness to the meeting of the bishop and his Italian visitor. Since the bishop and his secretary were both dead by the time we caught up with these events, I cannot tell you exactly what form the conversation took, but a perusal of the bishop's diaries for the year in question produced the following account, in the bishop's own hand, written on the back of the sheet for 20 June:

Had an interesting if inconclusive meeting with an Italian gentleman this morning. He was anxious to re-acquire the silver reliquary I bought in Naples in 1923. Our conversation was not of the easiest, because my Italian is negligible and his English nearly as bad, but, through a mixture of Italian,

English and Stringer's French, I think we made ourselves understood. He outlined the importance of the relic to his home village and the strict assignment that had been imposed on him by his family. He offered to buy it back, but the amount he proposed was well below its market value, in my estimation, and I declined his offer. There were other considerations in my mind: I was singularly attached to this humble medieval friar and his miraculous finger – call it an irrational and unworthy attachment, if you wish; I was not convinced by the gentleman's story, since he could produce no proof; I was deterred by the untruth in the newspaper advertisement which led to his visit; and I did not take to him personally: he struck me as untrustworthy, although I acknowledge that this could be my prejudice against southern Italians in general and Neapolitans in particular. I was told once that if it is not screwed down in Naples it will walk; and it will probably walk even if it is. However, my inability to accede to his request troubled me as being ungenerous, so I unbent to the extent of offering to consider bequeathing the reliquary to the village if none of my family should wish to retain it. He gave me a contact address, and there the matter was left. I shall consult my chaplain.

I owe the discovery of this note to Hewitt, who trawled through a cupboard looking for the appropriate diary.

(I discovered later that the bishop did consult his chaplain. I had occasion later, although I record my comments here, to ask Mr Skyner about the bishop's interest in relics. 'Oh,' he explained, 'Anglicans attribute no virtue to the relics themselves, which would smack of magic or superstition. No, we are moved to faith and prayer by the vivid memorials of people who are acknowledged to have lived out the Christian life. Relics prod our attachment to God.')

You will be wondering how we came to be interested in Toti Scifo. Let me go back a little. One of the matters which we determined should be further inquired into concerned any contact, and possible collusion, between Mrs Wyndham-Brookes and Adina Colver. When we returned to Hartlebury on the day following our conversation with Joel Colver, we requested straight away a meeting with the lady of the house – the *châtelaine*, I suppose we could call her. This time she received us in the salon, where we sat facing the windows on to the lawn. Mrs Wyndham-Brookes could clearly tell from my business-like attitude that this was no time for frivolous cups of tea: such were neither offered nor requested. I came bluntly to the point, beginning to be exasperated by my inability to grasp the ins and outs of the bishop's murder.

'Mrs Wyndham-Brookes,' I began, 'we are beginning to think that more than one person may have been involved in your husband's death, that there was collusion between a member of the resident household and an outsider. So far we have considered complicity between the bishop's chaplain and the almoner –'

'But, inspector, that's absurd! They dislike each other, for a start, and what on earth could they have in common that would persuade them to cooperate in my husband's death? Why dress it all up as an accident? In any case, where's your proof? No, inspector, your idea is completely absurd.'

'– and complicity between you and Adina Colver, Mrs Wyndham-Brookes.'

'Inspector, you take my breath away!' She bridled with a movement of her whole considerable body. 'This is fantastic. The very notion is utterly bizarre.' Her face took on a purple hue that gave ample expression to her indignation. She shook with the emotion of the moment. 'I and Adina Colver? Why, I hardly knew the woman! I've met her only once in my life, and I didn't take to her, in so far as our fleeting acquaintance allowed me to make a judgement at all. Inspector, I am outraged! You're taking unadulterated rubbish.'

I was unabashed by this outburst, having been the recipient of much worse in my life, not least from my own teenage sons, 'outraged' that I should suggest listening to Beethoven or reading Dickens. So I steamed on.

'I'm sorry you take such exception to my suggestion, but you must understand that I am only doing my duty. Adina Colver seemed to have wished your husband ill: if she could not have him back, nobody else should have him at all. I am not saying that she was rational, or even sane, in this feeling. We have information from her husband and from the writings in her desk that she attempted spells, and her presence at Hartlebury, purple plate and all, suggests that she was casting spells on the premises. However, this may have been a blind to disguise her entry into the castle. She might have taken advantage of visitors leaving; but she could also have received assistance from an insider. I put it to you, Mrs Wyndham-Brookes – ' my tone became masterful as I reached the climax of my peroration – 'that you had reasons to wish your husband dead and that you saw in the unbalanced Adina a means of putting your wishes into practice.'

'Inspector, I am speechless!' and for a few seconds this statement was no more than the truth. 'What possible reason could I have for wishing my husband dead?'

'You were planning to marry the Bishop of Chichester, who is a likely candidate as the next Archbishop of York.'

'What, Kenelm Boyde? You're joking, of course.'

'No, I'm not.'

'You got this – this gossip – off that despicable Stringer, didn't you, inspector? Admit it.'

'Yes, I admit it, but that doesn't make it untrue.'

'For crying out loud, inspector, Kenelm and I have been friends for years.'

'Yes, but according to Mr Stringer, your correspondence has been increasing in volume recently.'

'What a creep! I'm lost for words. What credence can you give to such a low form of life?'

'We can easily check in your rooms, Mrs Wyndham-Brookes, if you force us.'

This threat deflated our hostess. She remained silent for a while before resuming in more moderate tones.

'Very well, inspector, we *have* been corresponding more frequently of late. To tell you the truth, he was sympathetic to my increasing frustration with Giles's dilatory ways and talk of retirement. But murder? By all that's holy, you're concocting a complete and wonderful fiction. I tell you what, inspector, you'd be much better employed locating that unsavoury-looking stranger seen prowling about the grounds last week.'

'And what stranger would that be?' I inquired.

'Why, that man Mrs Wedlake spotted. That was her very word: unsavoury.'

'Why haven't we been told about him before?'

'You'll have to ask Mrs Wedlake that, inspector. I only found out this morning myself. If he's a foreigner, he's sure to be your murderer, you mark my words. Foreigners can't be trusted, not an inch.'

With that I decided to leave our conversation with Mrs Wyndham-Brookes, although I promised to speak with her again. She spoke once more.

'Before you see Mrs Wedlake, inspector, the chaplain has a small request, if you don't mind.'

'Yes?'

'Can you grant us full access to the bishop's study? There are papers in there that are apparently needed for today's conference.'

As I saw no reason to deny it, the request was granted.

We went off to the north wing to find the housekeeper. She was in her kitchen, preparing lunch for the expected visitors. She told us that a small party was invited to Hartlebury for eleven o'clock to finalise the arrangements for the bishops' funeral. Those present would comprise the widow and the bishop's chaplain in the first instance, then the almoner and the two archdeacons, the chancellor and the dean, and finally the undertaker. There was to be coffee at eleven, followed by lunch at half-past twelve, and tea at half-past three if it should be required. She had her work cut out, she assured me and Hewitt. I nodded to Sergeant Hewitt to conduct the conversation.

'We shan't keep you a moment, Mrs Wedlake,' he said amiably, and she smiled up at him. 'Please carry on.'

'I shall, if you don't mind, young man, but you ask me what you want, you know: it's no trouble.'

'We've just been told by Mrs Wyndham-Brookes – ' at the mention of whose name the housekeeper's nose visibly wrinkled – 'that you saw a strange man in the grounds last week. Why didn't you mention this before?'

'What, with all else that's been going on here the past few days? I can't remember everything, can I? I've enough to do without trawling back over every little incident from last week.'

'Please tell us what you saw.'

'I was going out to the dustbins in the yard, when out of the corner of my eye I saw a suspicious movement. A man had walked in off the drive and was standing at the bottom of the yard, but as soon as he saw me come out of the side-door, he turned round and disappeared. That's all there was to it.'

'And can you describe this man?'

'Below average height, moustache, broad in the shoulders, an

116

unmistakeable foreign look about him, if you take my meaning.'

'What sort of age?'

'I don't know: mid-thirties?'

'Had you seen him before?'

'No, not to my knowledge.'

'Has he been around again?'

'Well, if he has, I haven't seen him.'

We set out to find our mysterious foreign stranger.

THIRTEEN

A foreigner staying in the vicinity could not be difficult to trace. An Italian from a modest social background was unlikely to choose the more expensive country hotels or the bigger hotels in the city centre. He was, moreover, more than likely to have arrived by coach or train at Worcester in the first instance, if he had started from London. To Hewitt was therefore allotted the task of telephoning round all likely establishments, starting with the city, moving on to Kidderminster, then Stourport, then Droitwich. It took more than a few calls to locate him at the Oakleigh Guesthouse on the edge of Stourport, chosen, no doubt, because it was within walking distance of Hartlebury. We had perhaps underestimated the subtlety of our Italian visitor! Unfortunately we were told that he had signed out the previous Friday: going back home, he had said. We could imagine the gestures and broken English with which he had conveyed this intelligence. Still, we had a name and a home address, and I began to relish the prospect of a trip to Naples, which I had visited only once before: the Mediterranean sparkling in the still-hot late summer sunshine, the terraces of pretty villages on the hillsides surrounding the city, the oleanders and pomegranates, the olives and the eucalyptuses, the narrow roads twisting up the hill-sides, the rural people with their donkeys bearing on their laden backs the traditional Mediterranean crops, the rugged peasant faces staring out from under blue berets ... My vision expanded to take in the gardens of Caserta, the lava-splashed flanks of Vesuvius, the majestic and ageless temples at Paestum, the – Alas, my reverie was cut short by the news that our quarry had been laid up in hospital with two broken legs after a car accident, and it was at the Baldwin Lucy hospital at Stourport that we ran Mr Scifo to ground! He was frustrated, sorry for himself, bemused, but quite capable of being interviewed. I summoned up my best Italian from the darker recesses of what passes for my mind. Here before me lay - or rather sat, as we were in the day-room at the hospital - our latest suspect. I had considered the idea that what the bishop would not sell, Mr Scifo had decided to steal, and that the burglary had gone awry.

'Good morning, Mr Scifo, very sorry to hear about your accident': there was no reason for us to omit the customary pleasantries. I explained that we were investigating a murder, that we required his cooperation, that consular assistance could be provided if needed. (He looked a bit frightened at that!) Finally I invited him to give us an account of his movements the previous week. He did not seem apprehensive: just a little nervous, perhaps, but that could be attributed to his strange surroundings and, of course, to our commanding presence. Once he got into his stride, this is what he told us.

'It had become an obsession with me to recover for my village of Lorenzana, and for my family in particular, the relic of Blessed Giles which had been left behind in gift by the Franciscan brothers. The honour of our family required it if it could be achieved. Three years ago I came to England and spoke to the Bishop of Worcester, who was very polite but quite firm that he would not or could not hand the relic over to me there and then, as I had hoped. He let me see it – it is kept in his beautiful private chapel – so that I could satisfy myself that it was what I was looking for, but that is as far as he would go. Well, he did promise to consider bequeathing it to the village at his death, but that could be thirty years away, and in any case, I did not take that vague undertaking seriously. I therefore returned to Italy thwarted but undeterred (*ostacolato ma non scoraggiato*). I formulated a daring plan to steal the relic: history demanded it. I saved hard, and by this summer I had sufficient funds to finance a return to Hartlebury' (which he had great difficulty in pronouncing: it came out unaspirated, with a rolled r – two rolled r's! - an e that followed the r, and a u as in bureau - clearly quite a challenge!). 'I gave myself three days to carry out my audacious plan' (his very words: *il mio disegno audace*). 'My initial tasks were to discover the layout of the castle – and remember, I had already been inside, and that included the bishop's chapel – and the daily routine of the residents. I could not decide where best to hide, but eventually I hit on a spot amongst the trees in the field opposite the building, from which I could command a view of both the part of the drive leading into the car-park and the part that leads to the front of the castle. It was a long and weary vigil, I can assure you, inspector, but I did not flinch in my duty. By the Thursday night I was sure of my ground and determined to go ahead. Blessed Giles seemed to favour me in my venture, because at about eight o'clock, not long after I had settled down to await my moment, two cars drew up: late visitors! Excellent, I told myself, it could not be better. I could not be certain, from my vantage-point, where the bishop would receive his visitors. My goal was obviously the chapel, but they could be in the main hall, where I intended to enter. I therefore waited patiently until the visitors left. That was about ten o'clock, I suppose. I was then left in a quandary, which I had not, despite all my preparations, sufficiently considered, and for which Blessed Giles had not catered: if I took advantage of the unlocked front-door, I risked being seen by a member of the household; if, on the other hand, I waited too long, the door could be locked and my opportunity gone. Should I therefore go round to the side-door in the north wing and hope it was unlocked, or attempt to break in through a window at the back, which had been my original thought?' I sat aghast at the man's nerve, confessing to a member of Her Majesty's police-force his serious intention to break and enter! However, I said nothing.

'I also wondered whether I should not wait for the last lights on the upper floors of the castle to be turned off. As I sat there pondering,' he went on, oblivious of my concern, 'yet another visitor left the castle. At least, he couldn't have been exactly a visitor, because he left by the side-door.'

'Can you describe this man?' I asked.

'Well, I saw him at the wheel of his car as he left the yard, in the light of a lamp-stand on the corner: pinched features, as if he had been squeezed in some sort of press - a long thin nose, a chin that jutted forward, thin lips pursed in concentration, clean-shaven, quiet eyebrows, a clerical collar at his throat.' We instantly recognised our friend the bishop's secretary. Scifo eased himself up on his elbows, as if to relieve the pressure on his buttocks, his two legs stretched out in plaster and useless to assist him in the manoeuvre.

'What time would you say this was?'

'Um, half-past ten? Perhaps a little later.' His young face twitched with the effort of remembrance, his moustache wobbling.

'What did you do then?'

'Well, I waited some more, then went to the front door. It was still unlocked. I opened it with the utmost caution (*con tutta cautela*), heard no sound and crept in. There were a few dim lights on, but the place was quiet. I entered. I looked to my left through the salon and could see light under the door to the bishop's study. Holding my breath, and having no idea what I should do if I met someone, I made my way to the passage at the back of the building and so along to the chapel. I crept in noiselessly. There, I'm afraid, an unpleasant surprise awaited me: by the light of a solitary candle burning on the altar, I saw the bishop sitting up near the front! I was horrified, because I knew that my plan was scotched' (I translate *sventato*). 'This was a nightmare: all this way, all this preparation and all this waiting – for nothing! I couldn't think of anything to do: there was nowhere to hide, nowhere to wait; and just as I was wondering what my best course of action might be, the bishop, who must have heard something - my breathing, or the sound of my footsteps, although I was as quiet as a mouse – began to turn round; so I just bolted.'

I interrupted him: 'Are you sure it was the bishop?'

'Well, he had his back to me, but I suppose it was; yes, I'm sure it was.'

'Please go on.'

'Well, I hurried back to the hall as quickly and as quietly as I could, praying to Blessed Giles to save me from arrest, but just as I entered the hall, I heard someone in the salon. By this time I was getting really jumpy (*eccitato*). I knew the door from the salon into the hall was open, and I was frightened to be seen as I crossed the hall, so I moved quickly back into the corridor, closing the door again gently behind me, and all I could do was wait, tucked in by the side of a cupboard trying to conceal myself. After about half an hour, all seemed quiet, and I crept out from the passage into the hall again: no sound, nothing. Some dim lights still on. So I tiptoed across to the front door, only to find it locked! Would my troubles never end? *Beato Egidio, aiutami!* All I could think of doing was to make my way across the hall, through the north wing and out through the side door, which luckily was open. But there another unpleasant surprise awaited me! I couldn't believe my bad luck: where was Blessed Giles?'

When he paused, I became impatient: what further 'unpleasant surprise' could await him? 'Yes, please go on,' I ventured.

'I ran down the car-park, and then, just as I was turning into the drive, I bumped into a woman! Well, I was staggered (*scosso*): what could this person be doing wandering into the castle grounds at half-past eleven at night? Anyhow, we both looked utterly surprised. I backed off, but so did she, without a word. Where I was startled, I think she must have been both startled and frightened. I took advantage of this to run past her, and I ran most of the way back to my hotel! That's all I can tell you, inspector.' His head momentarily sank on to his chest. He looked up to meet me eye to eye.

'Now, young man,' I said masterfully, after clearing my throat and pushing my spectacles up the bridge of my nose, 'I don't disbelieve your story, but let me ask you a question: did you at any time go into the bishop's study?'

He looked genuinely surprised at the question.

'The bishop's study? Why should I do that, inspector? I wanted the relic, not a view of the inside of his study! No, I have told you the truth.'

More or less convinced in my mind that he was telling us the truth, I signalled to Hewitt, and we left the hospital, ruminating on the fantastic story: Hartlebury Castle was almost as busy at dead of night as it was in the middle of a working day!

Back at the station, I told Hewitt to prepare for a conference. There were two people conferring: he and I; and there were two items on the agenda: reconstruction of Thursday night's events and a wider consideration of the entire affair. When we were settled in my office, after the solemn production of a pot of tea and a plate of ginger nuts (I couldn't find any custard creams), I invited Hewitt to introduce the topics for discussion. This was no abdication of responsibility on my part: Hewitt was better at it than I, seeming to have a gift for cutting through complex data in order to arrange them in intelligible patterns; and in any case, his continued development as a detective officer required opportunities for initiative. Imagine the scene: a small, cramped, untidy office, containing a desk littered with papers, three chairs and a small sink, a cupboard and a filing-cabinet. Along one side of the desk sat the two conferencers (there cannot be such a word, can there? conferenciers? conferencees? no, sorry, it's gone): the older of the two, a big-boned man, somewhat loosely dressed, with thinning hair (although he is only forty-six years old), a large nose, spectacles, grey-green kindly eyes, thin lips and a humorous expression; the younger, fourteen years his junior, of smart appearance, smaller than his senior and less loosely constructed, with black hair, thick eyebrows and neat features and a permanent expression of intelligent alertness. What a combination, even though I do say it myself!

'Right, sir, Thursday night, with the castle seemingly as busy as Trafalgar Square. Apart from his lordship, there seem to have been nine people in or out of the castle, or in and out like figures on a Swiss clock. Excluding the bishop himself, the three resident members of the bishop's household were there all the time, although some of this may be presumption on our part: the episcopal consort, who presumably retired to bed at a normal hour – half-past ten, eleven o'clock? – and of whom we hear nothing more that night; the housekeeper, snug in her room in the north wing; and the chaplain, who was up star-gazing at midnight on account of an inability to sleep. There were then two legitimate visitors, summoned by his lordship for a consultation concerning feeling in the diocese: two out of the four evangelical clergymen who had been invited, Mr Wilkes and Mr Crabtree. They arrived at about eight and left at about ten, all perfectly regular and above board. Then two other members of the household were on the premises for some of the time. The first of these, the secretary Mr Stringer, entered the bishop's study shortly after the departure of Messrs Wilkes and Crabtree, apparently to entreat the bishop to reconsider his decision to sack him. According to Stringer himself, the meeting turned nasty, and Stringer killed the bishop; he then left the castle at a quarter to eleven. There is every reason to doubt at least part of this story, namely, the murder bit. The other member of the household active at Hartlebury that night was Mr Blake the almoner. Our informant, Mr Skyner, tells us that the almoner arrived as he, the chaplain, was getting himself some supper from the kitchen – shall we say nine o'clock? and in fact the almoner himself confirms that – and then left the premises at a little after midnight, having completed his work. He testifies to hearing sounds of others outside his room during his period of work – perhaps Mrs W-B or Mrs W getting themselves some supper. Now the almoner also states that, once outside the building, he noticed absolutely nothing untoward, even though he stood for a few minutes contemplating the moonlit scene in a reverie of wonderment and ecstatic communion with nature – unless that's an attempt to cover up for someone whom he *did* see.'

'Good heavens, sergeant, is everyone out to deceive us?'

'Could be, sir,' he said cheerfully. 'We now come to our two outsiders flitting round the castle or its grounds at dead of night, for no very savoury purpose. The first is the elegant and handsome Adina, whom unfortunately we had no occasion to meet in her lifetime. The picture there is that she had gone to the castle to cast a spell. That was on the Wednesday night. She stayed over, where doesn't matter, and returned on the Thursday night, either to repeat the spell or to murder the bishop, or both. Her presence that second night is confirmed firstly by her death in the stables, probably after finding herself unexpectedly stuck in the room where she had taken refuge, and secondly by our last visitor, the man with the broken legs, who bumped into her as he was fleeing the castle – before he had the misfortune to break his legs, of course.'

'Hewitt, cut out such feeble humour: it's a distraction.'

'Yessir, sorry, sir. And so to our last intruder, our Italian friend Toti. He lurks in shrubbery opposite the castle for two days before making his final bid. At eight on the Thursday evening he sees Messrs Wilkes and Crabtree arrive; at ten he sees them depart. He waits long enough to see the secretary depart at 10.45. He enters, goes to the chapel, is surprised and distressed to see the bishop there, retreats and hides for another half-hour because he has heard someone in the salon, before making for the car-park through the north wing. Let's place his departure at 11.30. On his way out, he encounters the lovely Adina. Once he is off the premises, frightened nearly out of his wits, the castle falls silent, except for the bishop, his unknown visitor, if there was one, and Adina. Now I hope you will agree, sir, that this reconstruction is extremely promising.'

'It is? Please explain.'

'Well, it enables us to exclude most of the suspects and to identify the culprit – almost.' He paused, beaming.

'Yes, well, get on with it: don't keep me in suspense!'

'Actually, it's probably not quite so simple as I suggest, but I do think matters are clearer, sir. First of all, the reconstruction enables us to eliminate, with every degree of probability, both Stringer and Adina.'

'How is that?'

'Stringer left the castle at 10.45 to return to his loving family. According to Toti, the bishop was still alive and praying in the chapel *after* that time: not long after, possibly, but at least the secretary had departed, and, according to the same Toti, the bishop was alive enough after his meeting with the secretary to make his way to the chapel and ensconce himself in prayer: hardly the actions of a corpse dripping with blood from a head wound. And to me that evidence seems reliable – sir.'

'Yes, all right; and Adina?'

'According to Toti, the front-door was locked when he tried to get out of the castle at half-past eleven. This is how I explain it. The bishop sees his evangelical visitors off the premises at ten; they leave by the front door. For some reason the bishop doesn't lock it at that moment; perhaps he just forgets, because it's not his usual duty. Alternatively, he dismisses the clergymen in his study, and they make their own way out of the castle. He returns to his study – if he has accompanied them to the front-door - and receives his secretary in audience. Then he decides to go to the chapel. As he's sitting in chapel, he thinks he hears a noise – we know it's Toti, creeping about in search of a sixteenth-century relic - remembers that he hasn't locked the door, goes to do so, taking a short-cut through his study and the salon, and then returns to his study in time to be murdered. That explains why Toti was able to gain entry through the front-door at 10.45 but found it locked at 11.30.'

I thought Hewitt looked quite pleased with himself at this point, so I decided to puncture his smugness.

'Tell me, then, how is it that Toti apparently didn't hear the front door being locked? He specifically told us that that discovery came as a nasty surprise to him.'

Unfazed, Hewitt continued effortlessly.

'There could be several reasons, sir. Remember, the door between the great hall and the corridor at the back was shut – I imagine - and it's quite a sturdy door. Or perhaps Toti was distracted at the precise moment by another noise in the castle or outside; perhaps he momentarily dozed off after all the excitement. Or perhaps the lock makes no noise. Or perhaps, being unfamiliar with the castle sounds, he failed to identify the noise.' His eyebrows went up questioningly.

'Very well, sergeant, carry on.'

'So if the front-door was locked before half-past eleven, and Adina was outside, I don't see how she could have got into the castle to murder his lordship. If she had done, there would have been no one to lock the front-door! How's that for a clever bit of reasoning, sir?'

'Yes, yes, very well. Please carry on.'

'Well, that's already two out of nine eliminated, sir! In my view we can also eliminate Mrs Wyndham-Brookes and Mrs Wedlake, neither of whom seems to have made a move; or at least they weren't seen, which is perhaps not quite the same thing. We shall bear them in mind. Messrs Wilkes and Crabtree left at ten, on their own testimony and as witnessed by Toti. Since they are effectively excluded, we're down from nine to three: not bad going, I think you'll agree, sir. That leaves two members of the household, Mr Skyner, who is resident, and Mr Blake, who lives off the premises, and the intruder Toti Scifo. For some reason I can't put my finger on, I believe Toti's story. In any case, how would he have the nous or know-how to set up the bishop's death as an accident? I just don't see it. Furthermore, what motive could he have for killing the bishop? If he had killed the bishop, he would have immediately returned to the chapel, stolen the relic and walked off with it. We can soon check, with a quick telephone-call to the castle, but my guess is that it's still *in situ*. Seven down, two to go. Skyner and Blake blame each other. Both had motive, opportunity and means. Could be either of them, or, as I hinted before, sir, both of them in it together, up to their homicidal little necks.'

'And the mysterious unknown visitor?'

'Ah, I was coming to him last, sir. We have the merest fragments of information: two in number, and both utterly insubstantial. The first is the presence of the Jacobus in the bishop's study. That it points to the presence of a visitor was your suggestion, sir, if memory serves me.' He coughed apologetically as a way of concealing his scepticism! 'The second is that a noise was heard in the salon at a little before eleven by Toti trying to make his way out of the castle unseen. We know from the bishop's diary that he had no further meeting arranged after the evangelical clergymen had gone –'

'But then their meeting wasn't in the diary, either,' I pointed out.

' – and in any case, it would have been very late to make another appointment, it seems to me. So who let X in, or did he simply make his way in through the front door? Why was he not seen by Toti? What was he doing in the salon? And had he gone by 11.30, when Toti tells us there was no noise anywhere in the building when he came to make his escape via the front-door? Big questions, sir.'

'According to your schedule of the night's events, sergeant, this stranger, X, male or female, must have arrived after 10.45, otherwise he or she would have been seen by Stringer exiting or by the watching Toti. Now Toti left his post – here we are estimating times a bit, but we shan't probably be far wrong – at 10.46. If we allow no more than five minutes for him to enter the castle, creep through the great hall, make his way to the chapel, stand a short while in the chapel and then make his way back to the hall, our X has a slot of five minutes – 10.46-10.51 – to make his or her entry; we know the front-door was still unlocked. He or she was still there at midnight and for some time afterwards, otherwise the vigilant and sleepless Mr Skyner, gazing up at the moon, would have seen him or her. If, on another supposition, the person in the salon overheard by Toti was not X but, say, Skyner going to have a word with the bishop in his study and waiting to be admitted, X could have arrived any time between 10.46 and midnight. Even if he saw Adina or she him, they would not necessarily have taken any notice of each other.

'And I'm afraid we need also to consider the possibility, which you yourself mooted, sergeant, of a conspiracy. You excluded Adina on the grounds that she couldn't have got into the castle after 11.30, because the front-door was by that time securely locked. What, however, if she was admitted to the castle by, say, Mrs W-B, and then, having murdered his lordship, made her own way out via the north wing? If X got in after 11.30, he too would have needed an accomplice to let him in, and that could be any one of the five people known to be still on the premises, namely, Mrs W-B, Mrs W, Mr Skyner and Mr Blake and, of course, the bishop himself.'

I took a few minutes to sketch in the following table:

person	timings (p.m.)	activity
Mrs Wyndham-Brookes	10.30-11.0	retires to bed(?)
Mrs Wedlake	10.30-11.0	retires to bed(?)
Messrs Wilkes and Crabtree	8.0-10.0	meeting with his lordship
Mr Stringer	10.0-10.45	meeting with his lordship
Mr Skyner	8.0-12 midnight	in his rooms
Mr Blake	9.0-12 midnight	working in his office
Adina	?	lurking; bumps into Toti 11.30
Toti	8.0-10.45 10.46-10.51 10.51-11.30 11.30	in hiding outside towards/in the chapel in hiding inside the house leaves; bumps into Adina
X	10.46-10.51 or 10.46-? ?	arrives leaves
	10.45-11.30	front-door is locked some time between these hours
	11.0-1.0 am	the bishop dies (pathologist's estimate: midnight)

I was not entirely convinced by this reconstruction, and Hewitt himself admitted that some of it was tentative. I felt we needed some more information, and to that end we returned to Hartlebury later that afternoon, Monday 5 September.

FOURTEEN

There were two people we had not yet interviewed to establish their movements on the night in question: the Mrs Bishop and the Mrs Housekeeper. Simon Stringer and Adina Colver, who could both have helped us materially, were, regrettably, beyond our reach. I was not sure that Messrs Chaplain and Almoner would be any more forthcoming at this stage – or perhaps they were already telling us no more than the 'simple truth miscall'd simplicity' of which our national bard speaks – although Toti might be persuaded to recall more details. Accordingly, early that afternoon, we first returned yet again to Hartlebury. Poking my head round the salon door, I asked Mrs W-B whether she would mind leaving her conference with the leading men of the diocese for just a few minutes, so that we could clear up a point that might be of some importance. If Mrs Wyndham-Brookes was waxing impatient with our comings and goings, she did not betray it. Armed with my morning table of the movements in the castle on the night of the bishop's death, we sat in the great hall, with her ladyship, and, after the necessary social preliminaries, I asked her straightforwardly for some information.

'I should like you, if you would, Mrs Wyndham-Brookes, to give us an account of your exact movements on the night of your husband's sad death.'

'So I'm still a suspect, am I?' she asked haughtily. 'Your interest in that stranger Mrs Wedlake saw came to nothing, then?'

'We have interviewed him and taken a long statement, but we are not convinced he was in any way responsible for the bishop's death.'

'Very well, inspector, if I have to. After tea – '

'We're interested only in the time after ten o'clock, Mrs Wyndham-

Brookes,' I said, hastening to cut short an irrelevant saga of petty domestic or personal details.

'I see. Well, at ten o'clock I was reading – in the library. You'll wish to know what I was reading, no doubt - '

'No, that won't be necessary, thank you.'

'At about a quarter to eleven – '

'I'm so sorry to interrupt yet again,' I said, but I could see that my intervention was unwelcome.

'What is it now, inspector?'

'Did you hear the bishop's visitors leaving, some time after ten, or anyone else arriving?'

'What, from the library? No, you can't hear anything that goes on in the front of the house from the library.'

'Thank you. Please continue.'

'Well, as I was saying' – and here she glared at me – 'I went along to our bedroom in the south wing. Since there was no sign of his lordship, I realised he must be working late and that I should therefore retire on my own, which I did. I suppose you now want details of my toilette?'

'No, that won't be necessary, thank you. Just tell us, however' (I was determined to keep Hewitt in the picture!) 'whether you heard anything else that night, anything at all.'

'No, nothing, inspector. Because I have a clear conscience, I fall asleep readily once I am in bed, and I sleep soundly.'

'Do you know who else was on the premises when you went to bed that night?'

'No, not precisely. I leave details of house-management to his lordship and the housekeeper once the working day has ended.' These words were uttered rather grandly.

Realising that the conversation was yielding us nothing of use, I brought it to an end. While Mrs Wyndham-Brookes returned to her meeting, Hewitt and I went off to the kitchen to see the housekeeper.

'Mrs Wedlake,' Hewitt said in dulcet tones, 'we're not disturbing you, I hope?'

'No, no, sergeant: always a pleasure to see you, young man.'

I had clearly dropped off the radar.

'We should appreciate it if you could spare us a few minutes of your time.'

'Certainly, certainly. Sit yourselves down. Sergeant, you sit here where I can see you as I finish the clearing up the lunch things. You don't mind, do you?'

She sat us at the large kitchen table – a traditional farmhouse table, with uncushioned chairs round it – and, momentarily interrupting her engagement with the pots and pans, bustled about with preparations for a cup of tea (I was glad to see).

'Right, sergeant, fire away,' she said at length.

'Mrs Wedlake - '

'It's Myrtle, sergeant.'

'Very well, Myrtle' (but I could tell that the word stuck in his throat!), 'would you tell us exactly what you did after ten o'clock on the night of his lordship's death.'

'You mean you haven't solved the case, yet?'

'No – but we're getting close!' Wishful thinking!

'Well, let me see. I was watching a bit of television. The programme ended at half ten, and I thought it was time I turned in for the night. Now you don't want to know *everything* I did, surely?' This was both arch and coy.

'No, no, Mrs – Myrtle, only important things.'

'But how do you know what's important, sergeant?'

'Well, we don't, of course. So, yes, please give us as much detail as you think could possibly be relevant.' He gave a faint sigh, probably – I hope! - inaudible to our hostess.

'Well, there I was, preparing myself for a good night's rest – and I won't go into details, sergeant, to spare your blushes - when I heard a noise in the yard. I went to the window, but it was only the secretary leaving the car-park. He had an old car, and it wouldn't start first time, so he had to try once or twice more to get the engine going. It was such a peaceful night, and the moon was so splendid, that I opened the window and spent a few minutes gazing out at the serene landscape.' (I thought that an unusual choice of words – but it turned out to be quite irrelevant!) 'I could feel a breeze, as I had on only a nightdress – oops, sorry, sergeant, shouldn't be telling you these things! – so I closed the window, climbed into bed, put out the light and went straight to sleep. There, that's what I did, and I hope it helps!'

It did not!

The other matter which had been on my mind, because I thought it needed further investigation, was the Jacobus volume. After the chaplain's initial remarks, on the morning of the discovery of the bishop's body, it had hardly figured in our inquiry, and I began to wonder why. If it was in any way unusual – its presence in the study, or the timing, or the possible fact that it was the bishop's killer who had asked to see it - it might hold a clue, and yet virtually nothing more had been said about it by anyone we had interviewed. Why was it in the bishop's study? Who had brought it down from the library? Should it feature in our investigation? Hewitt and I made our way to the bishop's study, taking a circuitous route to avoid interrupting whatever was afoot in the salon, but quickly discovered that the Jacobus had been moved. Supposing it had been replaced in the library, we repaired to that splendid apartment, but search as we might, there was no sign of it. In our frustration, I called the chaplain out of the meeting – I could imagine the grumblings inside, but our business was just as important as theirs! – and asked him whether he knew where the book might have gone to.

'Not the faintest idea, inspector. Look, is it really important? We're in the middle of a meeting!'

I picked up his annoyance at being disturbed – it would have taken a pachyderm not to – but was not a whit disconcerted. On the contrary, I was more determined than ever to run the book to ground. Realising that Hewitt and I could not on our own do justice to the many nooks and crannies in the castle, I telephoned for reinforcements, and in half an hour I had on the premises four able-bodied uniform interested in rummaging around the interior of Hartlebury Castle. Mrs Wyndham-Brookes making no demur, a warrant was unnecessary. Some rooms were quickly searched. For example, the great hall contains virtually no possible hiding place for a sizeable volume bound in leather; other rooms took more time. The library posed a problem. Hewitt and I had gone through the books as well as we could, but we had not looked to see whether the Jacobus might have been inserted somewhere on the shelves *behind* the books whose spines were visible.

Some might have counselled a single experienced dowser instead of six searchers. I was aware of arguments on both sides of the question; I had read of experiments constructed to test dowsing ability scientifically; I had read (popularising – anything else would have been beyond me) 'explanations' couched in psychological terms. I was also aware of the

Roman Catholic practice of praying to particular saints, notably St Anthony of Padua, for assistance in the search for lost objects. I had no firm views one way or the other: all I wished to do was to find a particular book, by whatever means. (I should probably have drawn the line at engaging a medium, at public expense, but I could probably not have given you a rational justification.) A nod in the direction of the paranormal was my instruction to the men to focus, mentally, on the object of our search. I described it in detail so that they could pick up its qualities and history. They were to think of an early printed volume, in Middle French (not that they were to open the book to find out!), published in 1476 in Lyons, size such and such, so many pages, each page divided into two columns; of the compiler, a mid-thirteenth-century Dominican friar, putting together, in his friary library or his own cell, with the aid of a flickering candle, accounts of 16 Old Testament personages, some 30 Christian feast-days and the lives of 200 saints; of the people who had read the work and used it to nurture their spiritual life; of the people who had handled that particular volume; of the bishop in whose study it had been found; of the holy men and women whose lives, however dressed up and fantastical, had found a lodging therein. I laid it on thick; nothing to be lost in doing so. I had envisaged searching the house and chapel without success and then moving into the outbuildings. In the event this was not necessary: the volume was found – if you are squeamish, you should perhaps consider turning the page now so as to avoid reading my next words – squeezed between a radiator and the wall on the first floor of the south wing: decidedly warm, but undamaged. It required little reflection to guess the culprit.

I dismissed the searchers, with thanks, and they were invited to the kitchen for tea and buns so that Mrs Wedlake could enjoy their company. The meeting had broken up and its participants departed. I requested a meeting – the third that day - with Mrs Wyndham-Brookes. She, Hewitt and I sat in the great hall, where we had first met, it seemed a very long time, but in fact only three and a bit days, before. The sky had clouded over and threatened rain. There was no noise that we could hear that Monday afternoon, either in the house or in the grounds. A scattering of lights in the immense room gave a slightly disturbing or sinister atmosphere; our hostess was noticeably muted.

'Mrs Wyndham-Brookes,' I said, 'I'm sorry to say you have led us a bit of a dance. I thought better of you.' The widow looked suitably mortified, hanging her head and fidgeting with her hands in her lap, but she said nothing. 'Please tell us about the Jacobus, from the beginning,' I continued.

'You must tell us the truth, partly because the truth is important, and partly because we are unlikely ever to clear up the mystery of your husband's death if we are denied it. We are not satisfied that you had nothing to do with your husband's death: now is your chance to clear yourself once for all.' We waited expectantly. The widow, sighing deeply, seemed on the verge of tears.

'I am ashamed, inspector, ashamed of myself. I have been childish and emotional; but I swear I had no part in Giles' death.'

'Take your time, Mrs Wyndham-Brookes. We should rather wait for the full story than have to suffer part-truths – or, even worse, untruths.'

'I have already told you of my attachment to Kenelm Boyde. It is a dishonourable attachment: it is betrayal of my husband, because he was a good man, but I just couldn't help myself. Kenelm is all that Giles wasn't: self-assured, sociable, assertive, a leader of men. Of course Giles was clever, I can't deny that. He was also holy: he had a feel for the things of God, the inner things; he was a man of prayer and reflection; but none of that was going to get him, or me, anywhere. As I grew older, less and less attractive – if that is possible – and less resilient, I began to hanker after a different life, a social importance superior to that of my sisters, not some half-mouldy retirement in a rural backwater.

'When I realised that my husband was dead, I rejoiced. I confess it, inspector – to my shame. I was sorry, of course, that his life ended so brutally; a good man should not die by the hand of an assassin; but I realised that at last I was free. I began to plan a new future for myself – as the wife of the Bishop of Chichester. I am a foolish old woman, inspector, but you are getting the truth, which is not, I regret, very glamorous and does not redound to my credit. The only life of St Kenelm I could find in the library was in a book of English saints called *A Compendium of English Hagiography* by Fulton Sharp. It is an old work, but I didn't mind that.'

The reader will pardon me if I here append the appropriate extract from the book so that you will properly understand Mrs Wyndham-Brookes' reasoning (or perhaps wishful thinking will convey my meaning better);

> St Kenelm (who may be entirely legendary) was the son of Kenulf, king of Mercia, the kingdom that covered most of central England, c.580-c.900. Kenelm ruled (briefly) in about 820. His elder sister Cynethrith, resenting his succession to the throne, persuaded his tutor to take him into the forest of Clent, east of Kidderminster, on pretence of hunting, and there behead him. The site of the murder is today marked by a chapel near Halesowen. The murder was discovered

miraculously: a brief letter (the text of which is given in Jacobus de Voragine's *Legenda Aurea* and which has been preserved in Rome as a holy relic) was dropped by a dove on the high altar of St Peter's basilica in Rome; but no one dared look for the body for fear of Queen Cynethrith's wrath. The sequel to the story is also miraculous, and again it is provided by Jacobus in the aforementioned volume. A poor widow had a single cow, a white one, which would go to pasture in the forest every day, rest at a particular spot, eat nothing, and yet return in the evening to give more milk than any other beast in the village. The cow marked the spot of Kenelm's hasty burial. There was a holy [did the author mean 'unholy'?] struggle between the shires of Worcester and Gloucester as to which should claim the body, and the Lord God, through a miraculous intervention, decided that Gloucestershire should claim the honours. The body was duly buried with great pomp at the Benedictine abbey of Winchcombe, the capital of Mercia. This, and many more wonders associated with the life of St Kenelm, are recounted by Jacobus: q.v.

Mrs Wyndham-Brookes continued.

'So, eager to know more, I went along to the library, that Friday night, to fetch the Jacobus, and then I suddenly remembered that it was in Giles' study, and that that was locked and sealed. I was frustrated. The account in Sharp whetted my appetite: here was a king, albeit a young one, the victim of evil forces, whose life and passing were marked by miraculous events and whose remains were found in Worcestershire but carried out of the county by divine fiat and buried in a glorious shrine. I saw in this story, fancifully, I daresay, a paradigm of my own future: I should marry a holy man of power and be transported out of the county to live in splendour.

'My moment came when I asked you to accede to the chaplain's request to open the study this morning. Before the meeting, I walked boldly into the study, using the annexe door, assured myself that the room was empty, seized the volume from the desk and made for my room in the south wing. As I climbed the stairs, the chaplain called me from below. I became flustered, as if caught red-handed in a felony, thrust the book out of sight behind a radiator, and came downstairs again to speak with the chaplain, trying to look nonchalant.

'Then this afternoon, when the chaplain returned to our meeting after you had called him out of it for a brief consultation, he told us simply that you had asked him whether he knew the present whereabouts of the Jacobus, and the meeting continued. I was agitated, but there seemed to be nothing that I could do. If I left the meeting on some pretext, in order to put the book back in the library, say, I could have bumped into you, inspector, or possibly Mrs Wedlake. So I stayed where I was, determined to retrieve the situation at the earliest opportunity. Unfortunately, you seemed obstinate in your search for the volume and had already taken steps to search the entire premises – with my agreement, but then I could hardly do otherwise. In next to no time, the castle was crawling with policemen. I sat tight: there was nothing else I could do. And that's all there is to it, inspector.'

'What I don't understand, Mrs Wyndham-Brookes,' I said in response to this rather pathetic story of budding hope and middle-aged love, 'is why you were afraid to be seen reading one of your own books! Who would have batted an eyelid?'

'The answer to that, inspector' – she continued to ignore Sergeant Hewitt entirely! – 'is simple. You had already thrown suspicion on me this morning: you virtually accused me of colluding with Adina Colver to murder my husband so that I could marry Kenelm. This is a preposterous supposition, I can assure you, with not a shred of truth in it, but I thought that if I were seen wandering round with the Jacobus, you would put two and two together and come up with five.'

'But how were we to know that you had retrieved the book in order to consult the fuller story of St Kenelm? You could have wanted it for any one of a dozen reasons.'

'Let me explain, inspector. When I went into Giles' study to get the book, I flicked through the index, found Kenelm, and turned the corner of the page down to mark the place. I slammed the book shut and made for my room, as I've told you. I had left an infallible indicator of my interest in Kenelm: who else would be suspected at this time? It would have been extremely fishy to be found consulting a life of Kenelm within hours of the bishop's murder, when it was known, apparently by all and sundry, that I had an interest in the Bishop of Chichester. If you had picked the book up, it would have fallen open of its own accord at the marked page; or you would have noticed a dog-ear and immediately wondered why it was there. It was vandalism on my part, but, as I said, I was all of a flutter at the time.'

This explanation did no more than justice to my powers of observation and deduction; I added it to the tally of the widow's virtues.

After her departure, Hewitt looked at me dolefully and shook his head.

'Much ado about nothing,' were his only words.

'Yes, I'm afraid so,' I answered. 'We have spent a lot of time chasing up the book, only to discover that it hasn't helped us at all in our investigation. It is still important, but its absence from the bishop's study this afternoon is not the important point. A little more detective work is required, I fear.'

'May I just ask you, sir, how you could be so sure that Mrs W-B was the one who hid the book behind the radiator?'

'It stood to reason, really. No one else had any business upstairs in the south wing, except for Mrs Wedlake, perhaps, and I couldn't see her skulking round with a book in medieval French. Anybody else would have had a mighty lot of explaining to do. Did you notice, by the way, how she seemed to ignore the caveat at the very beginning of the passage on St Kenelm? If he was legendary, so could her hopes be!'

It was back to the Jacobus for us.

FIFTEEN

I was a little daunted by the prospect of working our way through four columns of Middle French in Gothic print even before we considered the problem of its significance for us. Happily Hewitt hit on the idea of finding an English translation somewhere, and a few telephone calls located one at King's in the city. It was, such are the wonders of the modern policing system, magicked out to us in half an hour, and we began our analysis.

This is how we reasoned. The Jacobus found on the bishop's desk was not important as a book; it was important as a text. This was indicated by the presence of the bookmark in the chapter on Saint-Gilles:

Cxxv Interpretcion du nom faint gilles abbe Illes vault autant adire come fans terre et cler Car il eft dit de geos qui eft adire terre et de dian qui eft adire cler ou diuin Il ful fans terre par defprifant les chofes mondaines Il ful cler par enluminemant de fcience Diuin par amour diuine qui acfemble lamant auec celuiy qui eft ayme etc

The chaplain confirmed for us that the library at Hartlebury contained no English translation of the work; anyone wishing to consult Jacobus at the castle would therefore have, necessarily, to go to the incunabulum. Looking back, I now regretted not having had the volume checked for finger-prints; but I do not see how we could have known at the time that that might be important. I consoled myself with the thought that our mysterious visitor, X, need not have handled the book him or herself.

Now if it was the text that was important, it could be so for two reasons – we thought. Firstly, the bishop could have wished to point something out to his guest. Secondly, the guest could have wished to point something out to the bishop. Whether the pointing-out was by way of question or statement we could not, at that stage, be sure. We had already had several possible implications of the text pointed out to us in the early stages of our investigation, namely, that the murder was designed to prevent the bishop from moving forward to higher status in the Anglican Church (this was the relict's interpretation); that it showed contempt for the bishop's pusillanimity (Mr Stringer's view); that it was to prevent derailing of the process of rapprochement with Rome (Mr Rolfe's understanding). The first view would probably hint at an evangelical, the second and third at a Romanising, Anglican. All of them, to my mind, required a certain elasticity of interpretation of the Jacobus text. We isolated the following items from the English text:

- St Giles was high-born ('of noble lineage and royal kindred')
- he was Greek by birth
- he performed miracles:
  1. he cured a crippled beggar by giving him his coat
  2. he rid a snake of its venom (but apparently did nothing to save the man it bit!)
  3. he exorcised the demon from a monk
  4. he saved a ship's crew from shipwreck
  5. he cured a man who had been suffering fevers for three years
  6. he brought fertility to a desert place
  7. he was nourished on the milk of a hind
  8. his prayers saved the hind from its hunters
  9. an angel laid the king's hidden sin on the altar
  10. he raised a man from the dead
  11. he persuaded God to give two cypress gates fair passage from Rome to France
  12. he cured a lame man
  13. he foresaw a plot to destroy his monastery
  14. he foretold the time of his death.
- he was knowledgeable in the scriptures

- he was a man of prayer
- his dream was to be a hermit far from the haunts of men
- popularity was abhorrent to him
- he was kind to animals and had care of the environment
- he consorted with kings and withstood them
- his death was peaceful and holy

The fact that some, most or even all of this was legendary was neither here nor there. Our problem was to deduce from this material a possible motive for murder. One would have thought that the saint's many virtues (learning, humility, piety, prophecy, devotion to God, kindness to animals and so forth) would be grounds for admiration, not for condemnation. Had the bishop, on the other hand, failed to exemplify one or more of these virtues displayed in the life of his namesake? Was he at fault for not living up to his calling (as it were)? Unfortunately we knew already that any material could be twisted in more or less any direction: witness our three guides above. Hewitt appositely pointed out that the supposition that a person's life should be modelled on that of his or her name-saint is fanciful and unrealistic. Parents today do not choose names for their children on the basis of the virtues evinced by this or that saint, however much that may have been the original thought behind the custom of imposing a *Christian* name on infants. (It could, on the other hand, been a way of invoking the saint's protection in the child's life. My ignorance is displayed at every turn!) Who would have been genuinely swayed by the idea that the bishop had not lived up to the legendary merits and qualities of St Giles? Who would have taken it seriously? The fact of the matter is that, *if* the Jacobus was relevant at all, there must be a connection between the bishop's death and the feast of St Giles. I was coming increasingly to adopt the view that it was relevant. My reasoning was as follows. If the presumption was, as it might naturally have been, that the bishop could easily read Middle French in an abbreviated medieval printing style, the chaplain would not have remarked at all on the existence of one of the bishop's own books on his desk. The fact that the bishop could *not* read it – presuming that the chaplain was correct and not, for some devious reason of his own, deliberately leading us astray - pointed us ineluctably towards someone who could. That was the first thing. The second thing was the consultation of the book on the very feast of St Giles: this could not be coincidence. The third thing, more doubtful but worth consideration, was that the book had been left out for a purpose: its continued presence after the murder conveyed a message, even though that conflicted with the idea that the scene was dressed up as an accident. Against that was the supposition that the murderer simply had not had time or opportunity to return the book to the library. I asked Hewitt for his thoughts.

'Well, sir, I must admit that I am completely at sea at the moment. Despite my earlier euphoria, and clearly contradicting myself, I think we are now faced with five chief suspects. There's Mrs Wyndham-Brookes, who swears blind that she had nothing to do with her husband's death - a completely predictable response not to be taken seriously. She had means, motive and opportunity; and we have recently discovered that she could read Middle French, or at least enough of it to get the gist. We can't rule out a pact between her and Adina. Then there's the chaplain, possibly in cahoots with the almoner, and energetically pulling the wool over our eyes at every turn; the housekeeper, seeking revenge for threats to get rid of her – although what the book would have to do with it then is anybody's guess; the almoner, a rabid evangelical dismayed at the acceleration of moves to Rome spearheaded by his lordship; and finally Adina, exacting revenge for thwarted love and summoning mysterious powers by casting spells by moonlight. On the other hand, I believe we can eliminate the archdeacon, for the reason that we have had no indication that he was on the premises on the night in question – unless of course he is X! Similarly, the book would be totally irrelevant if the culprit were our wandering Neapolitan friend – which I doubt.'

'Just outline for me, if you would, sergeant,' I said, 'arguments in favour and against the venerable archdeacon's being our murderer.'

'Yes, sir.' He flicked over the pages of his note-book until he had come to the relevant page.

'The Venerable Mr Maddock Rolfe, archdeacon of Worcester,' he read. 'This is what we've got, sir,' he said with a glance in my direction before returning to his notes. 'He was reported to us as speaking out against the bishop's errors - not further defined, but presumably the errors associated with his convictions as an Anglo-Catholic. The archdeacon was also, if our informants are correct, stirring up feeling against the bishop in the diocese. He told us himself, in as many words - reading a bit between the lines, sir - that he resented his lordship's involvement in the talks with Rome. He drew our attention to the legendary life of St Giles. He admitted quite candidly that he wanted to see the bishop replaced with an evangelical. He also admitted that he had been at the castle on the day in question but had left at about seven. And finally he changed his story - possibly quite genuinely. At first he said he suspected the chaplain; then he told us that in his view the bishop's death was a pure accident. This is not a happy congeries of features.'

'No, quite, sergeant: not a happy – congeries – of features,' I repeated, rolling the word round in my mouth. 'So could he be X?'

'Well, sir, we know virtually nothing about X. We don't know when he or she arrived, but presumably between the short amount of time when Toti was not, so to speak, on duty at the top of the drive and the locking of the front-door. He asked to see, or he was shown, the Jacobus. He was overheard, if it was he, talking with the bishop in the study. And that's it! We don't know when he left. Now the archdeacon fits this profile, in that it would explain how he gained entry into the castle, where he spent time without being seen and how he was familiar with the layout of the building. It would explain his familiarity with the door of the bishop's study. He would certainly be capable of manufacturing a suitable piece of wire, and he could probably manage Middle French. One way to find out would be to ask his wife whether he was at home at the time in question.' He turned to me. 'Why haven't we thought of that before, sir?' I could not tell him, because I had no idea! A telephone-call produced the unsatisfactory answer that his wife was unsure: she and the children had been in bed, and she could not tell us for a certainty whether her husband was in the house or not. (Some people lead funny lives, do they not? The idea that Beth should not be sure whether I was in the house or not is comical!) I concluded that we needed to speak further with the archdeacon.

Accordingly, we left Hartlebury and made our way to The Old Palace in the city, where we imagined that the archdeacon would be hard at work either on final arrangements for the funeral or on matters arising out of the administration of the diocese, *sede vacante*. I have recorded for you earlier my initial impressions of Mr Rolfe – which were not favourable. I flatter myself that Hewitt and I make an imposing pair of detectives, able to instil into villains a due sense of the majesty of the law and of its inability to be deceived. Either, however, we were experiencing an off-day, or Mr Rolfe was exceptionally well-prepared to receive us, because he showed no nervousness whatever. On the contrary, he was almost genial, no doubt enjoying his role in the current events. We were ushered into his spacious office, offered refreshments (which naturally we accepted) and made to feel welcome. Feeling that this interview required the touch of the more experienced man, I told Hewitt that I should conduct it whilst he took notes: a fair division of labour!

'Mr Rolfe,' I began, 'please forgive this further intrusion on your time. There are still aspects of this case which puzzle us, and I hope you can spare us a few minutes to clear up at least some of them.'

'Fire away, inspector: I am most anxious to help in any way I can.'

'First of all, then, could you just confirm that you left Hartlebury at seven last Thursday evening and saw nothing odd on your way out?'

'Quite correct, inspector.'

'So you can't help us about a leather-bound book on the bishop's death?'

'No, not at all, sorry. I am 99% certain it was not on the bishop's desk when I left him.'

'Now you drew our attention to an event of St Giles' life which you thought might have a bearing on the bishop's death – this was before you changed your mind and came to regard his death as an accident. Have you had any further thoughts on the subject?'

'Well, I accept that you are now convinced that the death was murder, but, if it was murder, I think it had more to do with celebration of the feast of St Giles than with the saint's life.'

'Please explain, sir.'

'Right, inspector. Giles was a popular medieval saint: over 160 churches up and down the country and dozens of hospitals were dedicated to him. It's not surprising that special ways of celebrating his life developed. France and Spain were the same, I believe, although I can't speak for other European countries. So for example in London the custom grew up of allowing convicts on their way to Tyburn to stop at St Giles' Hospital, where they were presented with a bowl of ale called St Giles' Bowl: scant comfort, I should have thought, if you were about to suffer the ultimate penalty, but there you are. In Spain, shepherds came down from the hills with their best rams to attend ceremonies in honour of the saint. Nearer our own day, the Wiltshire village of Imber is open to past residents and visitors on St Giles' Day – I know, because I used to live near there; and so on. Now one popular way of celebrating the feast in England was to hold a fair, often extending to several days, and a particularly famous one, a three-day fair at Hartington in Derbyshire, was preceded by a week of preparation which took the form of a thorough – if it lasted a week, a very thorough! – cleaning of the house. So I put it to you, inspector, sergeant, that what our murderer was doing was to rid the Church of someone regarded as an encumbrance: a bit of spring-cleaning, if I may so phrase it. Rather crude, I grant you, but there you are.'

'And have you had any further thoughts on who this might be, sir?' Hewitt asked.

'Well, I have thought, of course, sergeant: the bishop's murder is naturally uppermost in our minds at the moment, but no, I can't say I've come to any firm conclusions on that point. If the bishop was getting in someone's way, or thought to be holding up important developments in the Church, or alternatively carrying forward developments that were better abandoned, well, we could be looking at virtually any committed Anglican of whatever persuasion, couldn't we?'

'A pity,' was Hewitt's only comment.

I toyed with the archdeacon's idea. Innumerable assassins have used spring-cleaning as a motive for murder, on the supposition that the victim's replacement will be less pernicious than the victim. Consider some victims of assassination in history: in the Old Testament and Apocrypha, Gedaliah and Holofernes; Julius Caesar, of course; Archduke Ferdinand, Abraham Lincoln, James Garfield, Jesse James, Mohandas Ghandi, President Kennedy; Henry III and Henry IV of France; Pope John Paul I (if some reports are to be believed); and other examples too numerous to mention. Some of these were perpetrated by the mentally ill; some by ideologues or military tacticians; some by hired killers for financial gain; some out of revenge. The underlying motive, however, is always (it seems to me), except in the case of mental illness, the perceived need (on the principal's part) to rid society of a harmful element. It is probably not possible to assess the effect of assassination: how could the historian ever decide, except in his or her fancy, how events might have developed if the attempt at assassination had failed? *Before* the deed, evidently, the assassin's calculation is that less evil will be committed by the murder than that committed by the victim if permitted to live, but one cannot, I thought, properly estimate the effect of the assassination on other claimants to the victim's position, on bystanders and observers, on interested parties, on the wider society. Frequently replacements have proved as destructive as the victim; or people regarded by history as good have had their influence curtailed. All in all, assassination is a gamble of colossal proportions, undertaken by people whose judgement is clouded, or at least partial, however sincere and earnest their motives.

The Bible is not really helpful, being such a violent book (or collection of books, I suppose one should say). For example, in the Second Book of Samuel alone, at least 100,000 people, plus innumerable others for whom no figures are given, are slaughtered on God's command, for no better reason than that they were not Israelites and objected to being overrun by the hotchpotch, fanatical and blood-thirsty armies of Saul and David. It was a mistake to resist, because victory over them simply gave the Israelites more fodder for their claim that they fought in God's name. It is true that a commandment, one of 613, forbids killing, but that seems, on a modern interpretation of the texts, to apply to peace-time, not warfare, so that the normal rules of civilised behaviour could be suspended in times of war if God so chose and commanded. There are arguments on both sides, I daresay, but only the New Testament is unequivocal in its affirmation of the value of the individual life, in all circumstances and whoever its owner. Even there, however, Christians have justified capital punishment – all a bit of a puzzle for a layman like myself.

I applied my haphazard considerations to the late Bishop of Worcester. Our inquiries had led us to accept that the bishop was a good man: learned, efficient, devout, tolerant, understanding, sympathetic, humble, a good husband, a competent administrator. Was his loss entirely deleterious? His only faults, in the minds of some, seem to have been a lack of ambition, a lack of ruthlessness or, in other terms, an excessive tolerance. How could anyone imagine that assassination was a cure for these ills? Humans are imperfect: we cannot expect all holders of positions of authority to be flawless in every respect. Were we therefore mistaken in interpreting the bishop's death as an assassination? Was it undertaken for motives that were much more personal and less public? Should we be looking elsewhere for our killer?

I ran over the suspects again in the light of this new thought. The widow's motives could, and probably would, have been personal: to rid herself of one husband in order to acquire another – nothing ideological in that. The chaplain, the almoner and the archdeacon could have objected to the bishop's choice of direction on ideological grounds, namely, either not moving to Rome fast enough or betraying the evangelical cause; so could the secretary, but he also, in his contorted mind, had a more personal motive – revelation of a felony that could cost him his job. The housekeeper's motive would, too, be personal: fear for her continued survival at the castle. Adina? distress at losing her former sweetheart. Toti? a burglary that went wrong. The chancellor? the two evangelical clergymen Wilkes and Crabtree? we had not even put them in the frame. And in each case we should have to fit in known facts: the presence of the Jacobus in the bishop's study, engineered, according to Mr Crabtree, late that Thursday evening, but whether by the bishop or by his 'guest', and for what motive, was uncertain; the setting-up of a scene of accidental death, which implied forward planning and familiarity with the lock on the study-door; knowledge, however rudimentary, of the household routine and of the castle lay-out; perhaps also knowledge that a weapon of death would be available in the bishop's study: otherwise the murder would be spontaneous, which hardly cohered with other facts of the case. Oh, dear!

SIXTEEN

We identified our killer that same evening, Monday, 5 September, within four days of his lordship's death: a record for me, I think, to whom my colleagues refer as Wavering Wickfield or Stalling Stanley, or, in a quite hilarious variation, Stop-Start Stanley (not very kind, is it?). The case was concluded amid such an exhausting flurry of remembrance and reasoning as almost to overwhelm my poor brain, and I shall tell you shortly how it came about. Firstly, however, there now follows the full, signed confession from the pen of the murderer, so that you may be in no doubt that the person we arrested was the right one.

'Now that the whole matter is over, I feel more comfortable about putting down, at Inspector Wickfield's request, the entire sequence of events that led me to murder Giles Wyndham-Brookes, Bishop of Worcester. I make no excuses; I merely explain, and that means I must start in my childhood. My parents were well-off but not wealthy. I was the middle of three children, and life was pleasant, except for one thing: because I was born with one leg shorter than the other, I limped, and a built-up shoe, whilst making walking easier, could not disguise the handicap. Uncertain what to do with my life, I embarked on a theology degree at King's in London, and I found that interesting, but, half-way through, I was diverted by a study of Thomas Aquinas, the great Italian scholar of the thirteenth century who figured marginally in our syllabus. Our tutor at the time, a Mr Gregory Willows, stressed how much Thomas' philosophy underpinned his theology and that the latter could not be understood without a knowledge of the Aristotelian metaphysics which

146

supported it. Thomas was a pioneer in the revival of Aristotle's philosophy, at a time when Platonism in its various forms held sway throughout Europe: a radical thinker. Karl Rahner, the German Jesuit theologian now in his 60s, of whom you may have heard, started with Thomistic philosophy and his own take on it before moving over to theology as the more interesting discipline. I reversed that journey. From being deeply caught up in theology, I came to believe that philosophy was the more basic, and therefore the more exciting, discipline, and from Thomas' highly distinctive and ordered theology I moved over to the philosophy on which it was based.

'Is there anything beyond what is accessible to our senses? If so, how could we ever know it? What instruments, so to speak, would be needed before we could gain an understanding of what exceeds the capacities of sight and touch, smell and hearing? Should we have to depend on intuition, which is not really assessable or exchangeable with that of others, or could we use our reason to argue to the structure of being itself? Plato had attempted to understand the phenomenon of change: how could a thing change and yet remain itself? How do we change and yet remain ourselves? In the process of change, what stays the same, what alters? Thomas discarded Plato's approach to these questions as having a basis not in reason but in guesswork, whereas Aristotle, he thought, had the merit of refusing to be guided by anything but his reason. Thomas liked reason because it was the divine gift that marked humans out from the rest of the animal kingdom and because it was the same for everyone. He accepted and developed Aristotle's metaphysics in a whole series of philosophical works, with gripping titles like *On Being and Essence* and *On the Principles of Nature*, commentaries on Aristotle, Proclus and Boethius, and individual chapters or sections of his theological works. He made a special study of angels, because he was interested in knowing what a purely spiritual being, one without the limitations of matter, would be like. He also pursued his philosophical studies into ethics, cosmology, natural theology and other branches.

'Now, for better or worse, Thomas never had an opportunity to apply any of his researches to practical matters; perhaps he had no wish to. He was never in a position of authority, either in his own order, the Dominicans, or in the medieval society of which he was a part. He spent his relatively short life as a man of learning, a scholar, a university teacher. I was increasingly attracted to a disciple of Thomas' who had the opportunity to influence public affairs as the superior general of his order (the Augustinians), as archbishop and as a writer of political treatises. Here was philosophy applied not to a further theoretical discipline but to real life. I refer to Giles of Rome, possibly a member of the powerful Colonna family which produced only one pope, Martin V, but was hugely influential for five centuries in the life of the empire and of the Church. Let me tell you a little about him, so that you may understand how he influenced my thought. I eventually wrote my doctoral thesis on him, of which you may possibly have heard, if medieval political philosophy is your forte: *The Abdication of a Pope: An Assessment of Giles of Rome's Position, based on a new critical edition of his* De renuntiatione papae (1959).

'Giles was born in Rome in about 1245 and died at Avignon, in southern France, in 1316, in his early seventies. Having entered the Augustinians in Rome, he was sent to Paris for his university studies. He stayed on to teach and write, getting involved in various controversies and public events, before being appointed superior-general of his order in 1292. In 1295 the pope named him Archbishop of Bourges, although the records reveal that he spent much of his time travelling in order to attend councils or to intervene in controversies. His writings cover various areas of philosophy (logic, ethics, politics, medical ethics and metaphysics), theology in all its ramifications and scriptural commentaries and include volumes of sermons. His collected works are in the process of being collected! He was later styled Doctor *Fundatissimus* – Most Secure Doctor, and his works became the basis of Augustinian studies. Of course only scholars read him today: his interest is almost purely historical, which is a pity, because he has ideas on the organisation and governance of the state which are still valid, in my view. It wouldn't harm our rulers to read his *De regimine principum!*

'You may now be wondering where all this is leading. I did not quite abandon my earlier interest in theology. What impressed me about Giles of Rome was his combination of scholarship and action. Here was a man not content with researching into the inner meaning of things but keen to bring his immense knowledge to bear on the problems of his time. Giles was a theologian and a philosopher who intervened in controversies between the pope and the emperor over their respective roles in ruling the empire, over the abdication of Pope Celestine V and the subsequent election of Boniface VIII, over the condemnations of the Knights Templar, John of Paris' eucharistic doctrine and Pierre Jean Olivi's alleged errors; and so on – all in all, a man of action the mainspring of which was his learning.

'One day I was consulting an encyclopaedia, to see whether I could locate more information on Giles' time in Paris, when, by accident, I began to read the entry on St Giles, a very much earlier and a quite different figure in medieval history - indeed, pre-medieval. I had no knowledge of him, indeed I don't think I had ever heard of him before, but my attention was caught immediately by his role as patron saint of cripples. I read on. The story included how he came to be himself crippled and how he cured cripples. It told of hospitals dedicated to his name. It gave a prayer for help for those who are crippled:

Domine Deus omnipotens, qui dedis servo tuo Aegidio curationis donum, exaudi intercessionem eius pro claudis, ut, te volente, de infirmitate eorum curati sint et deinde tecum habitent in lumine caelesti per omnia saecula saeculorum.

Lord God Almighty, who gave your servant Giles the gift of healing, hear with favour his intercession for those who are lame, so that, if it is your will, they may be cured of their infirmity and finally dwell with you in celestial light for ever.

I began to dream of a cure: foolish, perhaps, but everyone may dream. I had therefore moved from Thomas Aquinas the scholar, to his disciple Giles of Rome the scholar and man of action, to Saint Giles healer of the infirm – and thus to a consideration of my own position in the light of God's benevolence. My infirmity is nothing like so bad as those under which some people suffer, but I knew that it was an impediment to marriage: young people in the bloom of youth don't wish to get hitched to a hopalong figure who jerks about in an ungainly fashion and wears a built-up shoe. I knew I was over-sensitive; I knew that there were other difficulties preventing me from having a successful date; I knew also that anyone who takes any notice of lameness is not worth marrying. Not all of us, however, are so rational that our feelings have no influence on the way we think; and I don't exempt philosophers!

'When I moved to Worcester, I was encouraged – exhilarated - to learn that the bishop's name was Giles: a man of God in a position of authority. If he bore any similarity to his name-sake, he would be concerned for cripples, and you cannot imagine my delight when I learnt that, on the Feast of St Giles each year, he held a formal meal to which cripples of his acquaintance were invited. This year, to my astonishment and great pleasure, I was one of the chosen ones, and I duly took my place at table, a guest honoured, not pitied, much less despised, for my handicap. After the meal, which was held in the great hall at Hartlebury, the bishop was kind enough to have a few words with me. I asked him whether prayer is powerful enough to cure lameness, and he answered affirmatively.

"Look," he said, "why don't you come along to see me again tonight? I can't fit you in any time this afternoon or evening – appointments the whole time, you know – but we could have a chat about your problem later tonight. My last visitors leave at ten – and if they don't I shall eject them! – and we could sit down then and talk things over – that is, if you don't mind the late hour. We could try invoking St Giles' intercession on his feast day, and, although nothing may happen there and then, we can't do any harm by laying your infirmity before God. I am very sympathetic, you know."

'Well, I came away very happy and full of anticipation. I'm afraid that in my euphoria I drank rather more than I usually do, and by the time it came for me to leave home for Hartlebury, I had lost my usual decent restraint and quiet reserve. I asked myself what would happen if I wasn't cured. A very silly question, a normal person might have said, but I was keyed up and not in a mood to tolerate failure. I argued with myself that if the bishop – named after the patron-saint of cripples and a person of authority in the Church – could not cure me, he was a fraud. If he was a fraud, he didn't deserve to continue as Bishop of Worcester. He was merely masquerading as a man of God: he was not the genuine article. I should be his nemesis. Because I guessed that my appointment was not in his diary – and in any case, he probably didn't know my name – I could take risks.

'Because I wished to avoid leaving evidence at the castle, I parked my car a little way down the road and walked up to the front door. It was a little after ten, and I had seen two cars pass me at the bottom of the drive, which I guessed belonged to the bishop's last visitors. The front-door to the castle was ajar, so I went in. As I approached the bishop's study I heard voices in there, so I returned to the great hall and waited. I waited a good half-hour, almost beside myself with impatience, before a man came out and left through the hall, not noticing me slumped in an armchair. I thought I recognised, in the subdued lighting, Simon Stringer. Of course, I said nothing. I went up to the bishop's door, knocked and then answered his invitation to enter. He was as cordial as earlier that day, and I had every hope of a successful conclusion to our tête-à-tête. I could hardly wait.

'At first our conversation was general. He wanted to know about me, and my lameness, and how it affected my life. He wanted to hear about my job. He questioned me on my religious beliefs, and in particular on the intercession of the saints. He offered the use of a finger of Blessed Giles of Naples, if I believed that relics had any power, but I said that that was not what we had agreed on – I had never heard of Blessed Giles of Naples! – and in any case it was the Church's celebration of St Giles of Provence on that very day that was important to me. He then asked me how I wished to go about our little ritual.

"That's your department, my lord," I said. "You know far more about these things than I do."

"Oh, I just wished to be sure that we don't do anything you're not comfortable with."

So we chatted on a bit about the best format for our prayer, and the only condition I laid down, if "laid down" is the phrase I want, was that I wanted nothing to do with magic or superstition: we were going to celebrate the life of St Giles, and in that context we were going to petition God to have mercy on his poor servant – myself – as he had shown mercy to cripples during Giles' lifetime. To this end, I suggested a tangible contact with the saint: did the bishop have a *Life* of Giles that would focus our minds and express our solidarity with Christians of the *past?*

"I have," he said. "It's in the oldest book in our library, a collection of saints' lives published in 1476. Unfortunately it's in Middle French, and I've never succeeded in unravelling the print with any ease myself."

"Isn't there an English translation?"

"Oh, yes," he said, "but I lent it to a friend years ago, and I've never had it back. But don't worry, I know the saint's life almost off by heart."

"Right," I said, "would you mind very much fetching this book, my lord, and it will help focus our minds – or perhaps I should say *my* mind. It will be a tangible contact with the historical Church in its acceptance of the cult of St Giles."

Kindness itself, he disappeared for five minutes before returning with a weighty tome which he placed on the desk. I then asked him to run over the main events of the saint's life – for the second time in one day! – so that I could recollect myself in a suitable atmosphere of prayer. He tried to tell me that the purpose of prayer is not to alter God's mind or to sway the course of events, but to bend *our* will to what God knows is best for us; I was, in short, not to be disappointed if nothing happened; but of course I wasn't paying proper attention to that bit. We then knelt by the desk – why, I'm not quite sure, since prayers can be offered to God from any posture, but it was my irrational wish to kneel. We prayed in silence. Then solemnly, together, we recited the prayer to St Giles which I had copied out and brought with me. Nothing happened. I couldn't believe it. Nothing at all happened. We waited in silence. Then I suggested that we might try again. More silence. Another prayer. Still nothing.

"It's a con," I said, raging with disappointment. "The whole thing's a wash-out, a complete farce. God doesn't care about my leg, he doesn't care about me, I can go to hell for all I matter to him."

I was really worked up. I looked at the bishop, who had a sad smile on his face which I suppose was meant to express sympathy, but I was in no mood for sympathy. We had by this time risen to our feet, and I put into execution the manoeuvre I had practised in my mind. I hit him hard with the poker. I wiped the poker clean, arranged the body as if he had tripped over the rug, and then waited. I poked my head out of each study-door in turn and listened carefully. It can't have been much short of midnight by now, and all was deadly quiet.

'I realised, to my relief, that I probably had as much time as I needed. Although I had once tried to lock a door from the outside leaving the key inside, it was a long time ago, but I knew it was possible, using a stiff wire with four loops in it, and I had come prepared. Would you believe, it took me an hour of practising before I got it right? I can tell you that I was getting increasingly nervous and increasingly inclined to abandon the idea. I knew that the police would quickly conclude that it was murder if the doors were open – no pathologist would be deceived by the head-wound, and I convinced myself that my little scheme was worth a try, if only to mystify the police. Well, it worked eventually, and thankfully I left the castle behind me. I have no idea how Inspector Wickfield deduced that I was involved, but I offer my congratulations. I face life in prison with equanimity, since it cannot be worse than my life outside.'

'So, sir,' Hewitt said, 'how did you make your deduction – a quite brilliant piece of detective work, if I may say so, sir!'

'Yes, thank you, sergeant, you may say so, but between you and me – and for heaven's sake, don't tell Falconer: I'll think of some little story to deceive the poor soul - it was more the result of a prompt from Beth than of any brilliant reasoning on my part. It happened like this. We were sitting over our usual cup of tea after supper, and, again as usual, I was reading through my notes on a baffling case for the umpteenth time, looking for the crucial clue – perhaps – that had hitherto eluded us. Beth was reading the evening paper. Our conversation went something like this. It is bizarre that so random a conversation opened my eyes to the solution of the Hartlebury mystery.

"What say you we go to see this new film *Jemima + Johnny?*" she piped up.

"What's it about?" I asked.

"The 1958 Notting Hill riots. It's a film in the Free Cinema tradition, according to this critic, in a 'gritty, realist' style, filmed with hand-held cameras, in non-sync sound, whatever that is, and so on. Sounds OK. We could do with an evening out.'

"Are race riots quite our thing?" I asked dubiously.

"Of course," Beth said firmly. "You need educating, Stan: it'd help root out all your prejudices."

"I am completely unprejudiced," I retorted. "In fact, I'm probably the least prejudiced person you have ever encountered in your life. I am quite capable of discriminating between a gang of Jamaican thugs invading the Worcestershire underworld and genuine asylum-seekers or immigrants intent on improving their prospects in life and on contributing to their adoptive country. I have no hang-ups about immigration, from whatever source." I became heated. "Why," I added proudly, "I could name you a dozen immigrants who have become part of British history and whose contribution I value: Holbein, Hollar, Handel, Brunel, Conrad, Naipaul, Hornung – "

"Which reminds me," Beth said, with breathtaking disregard for my eloquence, "I've just finished Hornung's *Dead Men Tell No Tales*: I shall pass it over, as you might enjoy it. An early work, before he got hooked on Raffles. Plenty of story and adventure. I think you might find it a useful break in the middle of the works of Racine, or whatever it is you're engaged on at the moment."

"*Dead Men Tell No Tales*, you say," I answered meditatively. "I wonder."

With that I scurried back to my notes. Do you remember what Carson Heywood said when we asked him whether Simon Stringer mentioned the presence on the bishop's desk of a valuable volume from the library?

'No, I'm afraid I don't, sir.'

'Well, I'm glad to say I made a note of it at the time.' I flipped back through my note-book. 'His exact words were, "Only to the extent of saying that he hadn't seen it there earlier in the day".'

'Yes, sir,' Hewitt said dutifully. 'I'm not quite sure … '

'I shall have to spell this out to you, sergeant, I can see. You will remember that at the start of the investigation – all of four days ago – we had no idea who had brought the Jacobus down to the study or when, let alone why. We have now discovered that it was the bishop himself who brought it down, at his late visitor's request. Whatever the precise time was, it was certainly after 10.50, when the bishop's final conversation of his life, the prayer-cum-failed-healing session in the study, had started; probably well after 11.00. We know for certain that Simon Stringer left the castle at 10.45. He told us that himself, in his suicide letter; Mrs Wedlake saw him go; and so did Toti. It is inconceivable that he returned a little while later to be the bishop's last visitor of the day. It follows as sure as Monday follows Sunday that Stringer could not have seen the Jacobus in the bishop's study that day. It follows equally surely that our informant, who says he did, was lying: over-confident that *Dead Men Tell No Tales*, he slipped up in trying to make the events of that evening sound natural and in casting Stringer as the murderer. Now I've explained it all, sergeant, it doesn't sound particularly clever, does it? You forced me to it, and I've lost out!'

'So why didn't Toti see him?'

'Simply because the two evangelical clergymen were in cars. They would have been between Toti and the visitor we nominated X, who, we have now been told, was on foot. Heywood would be making no noise, and the cars' headlights would have dazzled our young Italian watcher. With neither sight nor sound to guide him, Toti simply didn't see the bishop's last visitor. X had only to dodge behind one of the gatehouses to avoid the headlights, so the visitors leaving wouldn't have seen him either.'

'And we were completely wrong deducing that, because there was a book-mark in the chapter on St Giles, the Jacobus was brought down to be read, not simply as a volume.'

'Yes, I'm afraid I was misled. Still, we got there in the end,' I sighed with satisfaction.

154

'And Blessed Giles of Lorenzana, Brother Giles of Assisi and Doctor Giles of Rome were all completely irrelevant.'

'Yes, but we couldn't know that, could we? In any case, it's all been good for your education, sergeant. Furthermore, Heywood's screed clarifies one or two other points for us.'

'For example?'

'For example, it explains why Toti told us that when he came out of hiding, if squeezing in beside a cupboard can be counted as hiding, he heard nothing from the direction of the bishop's study: the bishop and Heywood were engaged in silent prayer. And it has given me a further thought about poor Adina: when her spell failed to work, she simply gave up; she died of a broken heart, poor soul. She was quite innocent of designs on her old lover's life. And it points up a mistake I made in our reconstruction: Heywood arrived on foot, whereas I was presuming that X, like every other visitor to the castle, arrived in a car. That just shows how much the car has caught hold of our imagination in 1960s' Britain.'

'There's another thing, sir: we wondered at the time why Mr Stringer gave us no details of the murder and apparently expected us to accept without demur his ability to lock the study-door from the outside while leaving the key on the inside. Why are we believing Heywood so readily?'

'Well, partly because his confession is comprehensively convincing; but also consider this: anyone with any interest in locked-room mysteries and the literature to which it has given rise is going to want at some stage to have a go himself. I don't find it in the least incredible that our philosophical friend should have wondered whether the usual methods employed in detective fiction work in practice and that he should himself have experimented at some stage. After all,' I added after a slight pause, 'I was guilty of this myself in my youth. It comes of having a lively and inquiring mind, you know.'

Lightning Source UK Ltd.
Milton Keynes UK
03 March 2010
150845UK00001B/94/P